MERMAIDS FOR ATTILA

MERMAIDS *for* ATTILA

Stories by
Jacques Servin

Boulder • Normal

First edition
First printing, 1991

Published by Illinois State University and Fiction Collective Two with support given by Illinois State University President's Discretionary Fund, the English Department Publications Center of the University of Colorado at Boulder, the National Endowment for the Arts, the Illinois Arts Council, and the Teachers & Writers Collaborative of New York

Address all inquiries to: Fiction Collective Two, c/o English Department, Illinois State University, Normal, Illinois 61761

Mermaids for Attila
  Jacques Servin

ISBN: 0-932511-50-3 (cloth)
ISBN: 0-932511-51-1 (paper)

Manufactured in the United States of America
Distributed by the Talman Company
Typesetting and design by Jean C. Lee, Gail Gaboda
Cover/Jacket design: Dave LaFleur

For my parents, for Freda, and for John Brillhart

Contents

What Will the Army Men Do?   11

War Memorial World   13

Luck: A New York Fairy Tale   15

Life (A Porn Story)   17

Still Life With Death (Texas)   19

"I was living in the gay rodeo…"   21

Mighty Fine Baby From Where?   23

An Account of the Respite   25

Manure   27

"Ministry…"   29

Interesting Exhibit   31

Fire in the Crop   35

Modern World Problems Acknowledged By Us   37

Regarding the Uncustomary Events of 1989 Which
   Occurred Here and There Around Northern Europe   39

Great Sea Occurrence   43

Still Life With Disaster (U.S.)   47

The Dump-Man   51

Oonchi Has a Bad Day   53

Memories of States 1938 (Launch, Epiphany, Sphincter)   57

We Managed To Do Quite a Bit   61

"The method of distillery was remarkable but we angled down…"   63

Home Fat Plot   65

The Zoologist   67

The Bad Thing 71

City Story 73

A History of the Wealthy World 75

Bad Day on the Moon 77

Revolution's Moments 79

"My country, Peru…" 81

An Aphrodisiac History of the Family 83

Unusual Sight 85

Grace 87

Detachment 89

The Appropriate Endeavor 91

Escape From Paris 93

Tia Carro and Her Babies 95

Easy Time 97

Adjective Death in the West 99

A Wisdom Tale 103

Coarse Home Event 105

The Glorious Contribution of Academia
    to the Twenty-Fourth Century 107

Devil in the Bathroom 111

The Turk and the Virus 113

"At the end, a mighty ovation…" 115

Ex 117

Angry Suburb Story 119

Spooky Days of the Wide-Eyed 121

Byway Idylls 123

ACKNOWLEDGMENTS

Acknowledgment is made to the publications in which these stories first appeared:

"War Memorial World," *Fiction International*
"Luck: A New York Fairy Tale," *Witness*
"Life (A Porn Story)," "Still Life With Death (Texas)," and "The Turk and the Virus," *Colorado North Review*
"I was living in the gay radio...," "Memories of States 1938 (Launch, Epiphany, Sphincter)," "A History of the Wealthy World," "My country, Peru...," "Escape From Paris," and "At the end, a mighty ovation...," *Exquisite Corpse*
"An Account of the Respite," *Fine Madness*
"Modern World Problems Acknowledged By Us," and "Home Fat Plot," *New American Writing*
"Great Sea Occurrence," *Australian Short Stories*
"Still Life With Disaster (U.S.)," *An Illuminated History of the Future*
"Oonchi Has a Bad Day" and "Byway Idylls," *Central Park*
"We Managed To Do Quite a Bit," *Hanging Loose*
"The method of distillery was remarkable but we angled down...," *Carrionflower Writ*
"An Aphrodisiac History of the Family," *The Salmon*
"Spooky Days of the Wide-Eyed," *Processed World*

WHAT WILL THE ARMY MEN DO?

A tiny spring of madness—oh so tiny!—elfin, in fact, with a cute propensity to declarations of greed—but tenacious, and that is not easy to take—annoyed our three hundred languidest generals, back-arching colonels, dust-lunched lieutenants and more to the point with gathering charms and steel they marched right up to the towering rock, the face of which was impregnable, sang hymns, and commenced a frenzied drilling. A great and responsible show, and singing was not stopped:

"O drill—mammocking rock—to the core of the rock—
The shrapnel chivying thoughts to fear—
Terrific, I say—terrific, men—terrific...."

Oh, the wives back home, rounding up soup in the tenement streets, running up bills with appliance stores, lunching on nuts at Beckman's, crushing their fingers in Beckman's machine, cursing Beckman, cheating with Beckman, lunching on Beckman's vitals, grouping mean around Beckman, getting clever with Beckman, leaving paste from the list of commodities needed....

Afterward, breakfast. "*Idiotas*," said the visitor, "seldom hold forth on the virtues of marriage fidelity." Grouping around him now were the colonels, strappingest privates, and bystanders: bikini-wrestling men of complexion, men with sores on their ears, electric men with the gall to eulogize charge—thinking men, men with thoughts growing softly, softly into razor-sharp lines:

Sad! Sad! Here in our country, here among men like us, here, thoughts of correctness and doom so rife in our culture—here, this man is alone, alone with his forms of self-mutilation so healthy, the physicists tell us, for growth of good habits of love and revenge, crust and fierce corn....

"And so," the visitor finished, "we must, must try to look back to the days of sable-haired youths in their coats of iron yelling sing-song desire to girls of terrible pallor in hopes of eternal pleasure. Not moments of bliss. Eternal pleasure. A very long thing."

"Hunk," a wife said, "give teeth to that wish."

Hats were removed. Ties were concealed. Heaviest medals were put in cheap socks. A luncheon was dropped in the bower.

An excellent scene. The men were home.

A grouping of sea birds sang in a warble, Ima Sumac in polished granite—

"Drills

Drills were the way of the day

Drills

Drills toted down to the quay

Drills

Drill-parts by ocean-brine lapped

Men

Smiles with ignorance capped."

Suddenly, three hundred men of rank and pus were as children, randomly tucked and prodded by wives, urged to the edge (or given what? asked for what? touchingest gait of malarial death in the semblance of gains...)—and there, at the edge, three hundred wives were trucks of remorse and doodle-hand flexion and three hundred men were packed off with kicks to the loosenesses of wrack and curl, and madness was given the message:

"come and change our sports

send our greetings to all springs

great is the time of"

WAR MEMORIAL WORLD

At the entrance, one hundred guards in various states of squashedness. Mo, the tallest, exhibits concave rib cage. "How did it happen, Mo?" "I leapt into military situation with my hoedown still tapping its vim in my ear—ka-blooey!" We get enough of the picture. His friend Alexis is revering something small and metallic on the floor. "Come closer," he says to our pleated-trousered leg. "This war," he says, "involved a cost of three thousand bushels of aught-aught-six, and a good many lives of my comrades gentle in brooks and the fairs we got so very, very used to." Where is his face? "In the sixth month of it," he says, "the bloodhounds contrived to undo me."

"Tell us about your face."

"This war," he says, "involved the throwing of abundant livestock into the rivers of Hell. We were marching and growing a certain panache when clummo! the river swelled and only by remarching all the way back to the font could we have repaired our situation, so clummo! we threw a farmful of livestock into it. Boom! The river stopped. Now who says there ain't no such thing as sympathetic magic?"

He sees us gesturing maniacally at our face.

"And then the aught-aught-six ran out and the enemy revamped its nightcamps to accord with the solemn vow of Astarte, its god, to please allow its subjects to decamp with less excess when near the enemy troops, meaning us...."

We throw little peas at his face.

"At that point the enemy blew up my face."

We push past the entrance guards (one hundred and ten, in fact) and follow the signs to the Boulevard of the Goosenecks. This is a place where friendly ex-soldiers can celebrate the time before howitzers, planes, fathers, and landed-gentry memorials.

LUCK: A NEW YORK FAIRY TALE

The man didn't think of the world as fearsome, not usually, but he read a lot of books and spent a lot of time in lines. In line he thought about the Soviets. The books he read were all about crime.

One day, he shattered all of the windows in his tenth-floor apartment by tapping a long time on their embrasures with a little brown ball-peen hammer.

He couldn't well afford to buy new ones, so for several days the man slept bundled up beneath all the blankets he had. At night he dreamt mostly of food piled high but in the mornings he didn't eat till noon.

Finally he cleaned up the glass with a neighbor's broom and applied to the credit union for a loan. He rearranged his furniture and hoped it wouldn't rain too much.

Mary was ugly in the rain. At lunch she told the man that she and Paul, to whom she was engaged, were applying for splendid grants to go study jackals in Algeria, and both were pretty confident of their chances. The man nodded attractively, though the very word "jackal" made him shiver.

The loan came through and the man replaced his windows. Paul and Mary came over for lunch. Paul, who danced on the side, stepped on some glass and worked at it with tweezers while the others ate. "Well!" He held up a tiny red thing in the tweezers; now he could eat too. Mary passed the salt and the man steadied Paul as he slipped on his thong.

The man, ribald, told a little story about the stock market, something he had read that really explained the where and whither of it all. His friends left. He felt a little crazy.

• • •

Mary had a bad accident and Paul gave up his grant. The man spent part of the next day at a museum, looking at pictures, reading a book, and staring at a guard. The guard began staring back and the man left after dramatically inspecting some of the larger works.

Mary was outside his door, sobbing. The man put a calm hand on her chair and fumbled for his keys. They made love on the couch because Paul had decided to leave her after all. Then she started emitting tight, quick wails from her throat and the man had to give her sleeping pills to make her stop.

"Puh," the man said to himself after she had stopped wailing. Usually he was quite voluble, but there seemed to be something important going on here. He washed the dishes and mopped the floor. That night he dreamt of food piled high.

In the morning he went with Mary to the same museum and showed her some paintings he remembered. He showed her a painting with jackals. She seemed very interested, he noticed, and the things she had to say were subtle. Outside, as he was pushing her toward an ice cream stand, she began to sob again. "Now," the man said. "That. Can't I. Prick."

That night he called Paul, who said nothing. There was nothing to say, Paul said. The man told Paul he thought Paul was all right but Paul didn't answer and the man felt a little crazy again. But Mary sobbed and gripped his shoulder and eventually the man fixed some terribly sweet tea for them both.

Then the man, who had lost a great deal in life, fell into a routine whose focal point was Mary. Mary received an inheritance. Two years later, their names appeared in *The New York Times*.

LIFE (A PORN STORY)

1. Bountiful trouble

Bloodhounds! Infernal bloodhounds! By the dozen, assuming positions around the foreman! The foreman, donning disguises one by one, one by one, plumber electrician bloodhound vampire, but none succeeds in dispelling the bloodhounds. Handy is not a steel blade with a rubber handle, nor electric socks for the cunning of foot, nor sixteen thugs with bloodhound-dispersant aroma. Instead the foreman is all alone, and the workers, building a seven-story factory, wend wrenches with thrust and joy, ignoring the bloodhounds, perhaps just "chancing the fuss"!

2. Victory

There is a certain dusk, the bloodhounds notice, a dusk not characteristic of the ordinary working-time of a foreman's crew, and they worry about wages and union-influenced overtime bonus, and they look at the yellow foreman and notice a queer aroma of baked salami and suddenly the room is dark. It is in France and the bloodhounds are gasping for air in the soft night air of Limoges, a town renowned for porcelain, and the foreman is reading a phrasebook with the perfect back of a well-directed attentionwise Frenchman, curved just enough to be French-in-attention but not enough to be Italian-at-work, and the foreman considers himself quite lucky, but the bloodhounds are sore, they are gagging on the soft night air of Limoges, they move to Brussels...

3. Poverty (later)

The foreman is selling his trinkets hard by the plovers in the Belgian National World of Birds, trinkets by the dozen pass from his hands but it is important to realize the trinkets are pretty, so pretty the bloodhounds inspect them for flaws (find none), and the foreman sings a ditty of severe poverty hard by the plovers in the Belgian National World of Birds, and Maria Callas opens her heart to him, recounting endless paramours dressed in satin, masochists all, and all the great singers pop up in his mind, he cannot decide which, he cannot stand still, he scratches the folds of his anatomy and the bloodhounds are charming the insects with their prattle, the same insects who would ordinarily be scampering from them in fear...

4. Nothing wrong with tranquility

"I am safe," the foreman speaks in the desert, his toe designing arabesques, as the bloodhounds fall from the sky like entertaining confetti. The world is over, all over, all done, and the foreman is safe. The sky rains down its miraculous bloodhounds, replacing the web of information that never stops, and the foreman gazes with perfect solemnity at the clear, smooth expanse of void that he knows is the darkness of space right beyond the ionosphere of his planet, the earth.

STILL LIFE WITH DEATH (TEXAS)

Breeziness in the heart of Texas. John, tall and not bow-legged, greets his friend Mortimer. Mortimer is fifty-five and responds with a rousing halloo. Mortimer speaks that way, in halloos, out of habit born of indecision: a left turn in graduate school took him to medicine. And now he's a doctor. John looks on with the sturdiness of well-lived youth, and responds with a rousing double nod. Mortimer, stuck in his role, his role, responds with questions on the environment, political achievements as of late, and standards of efficiency. They are friends, John and Mortimer (and I prefer John), but also coworkers. That complicates matters somewhat, and simplifies matters too, but roles are roles and John and Mortimer live on.

Next day, breeziness in the heart of Texas. John has completed a *satisfactory inspection* of the lower-downs, inbreds as he calls them (and you thought he was educated!), and Mortimer responds with a rousing halloo. Mortimer must feel pleasure at the presence in the heart of Texas of such a fine constellation of attributes, all in his work force. But he must also feel pain at the distance from himself of certain benefits of having John, young John, in the echelons, benefits accruing to his coworker Sandy, not to Mortimer. John, for his part, sands his profile, but he cannot sand enough, and it is not his profile that is wholly to blame. He has a generous soul (I prefer him to Mortimer).

It is a general error, this situational triangle, an error I deplore, but life continues in Texas and the sky rains down its miraculous web of information. Endlessly, twenty-four hours a day.

Sandy appears, a sea of bounce. "Ahoy my delightful machines!" he calls in the morning. "But not too delightful," a lower voice adds, his own. "But not too delightful," Sandy calls out. His coworkers hear him, but they in their cubicles are private, and John is slurping tomato from his typewriter and Mortimer's all-around in a shame trance, so no one thinks to mock Sandy, and this in other permutations is the general situation with the three and the situation continues, and no one ever mocks Sandy. The environment grows so efficient that Sandy becomes a thoroughgoing yelp of efficiency and John and Mortimer listen in. "Confound it," Sandy says, "I cannot find the battery!" John fingers pencils, wants the night to arrive, grazes old Mortimer with the cushions of air on his anxious palms. (Sandy is attentive and friendly. Mortimer will not understand John's love. He ends by not understanding Sandy's either. Perhaps some things are too mysterious overall.)

At night, winding-down in the heart of Texas. Sandy prepares a scotch and listens to John recount the horrors he sees in the breezy office. There is love between them, and a good deal of out-and-out exploitation, and there is room for a little enthusiasm—John is young. An enormous portrait of Mortimer hangs above the sofa and they play a love game in which they splash it with scotch! The very next day, Mortimer dies.

Horror in the Texas workplace!

I was living in the gay rodeo, heavy round-up of sensational performances, Gusty Perceiver and Blam Hart and Curtsy Stackless Aye-Aye, and right in the middle I fell in love with the handsomest, most lovely assortment of features the world has known: connubial glee assailed the gay rodeo. His name was Johnny, a freezing fellow, consumed by wants and loves. We were lovers and just as it was happening, he for me and I for him, I decided to check this moment into permanence and with it found a society, later, of true love, starting with this.

I am peeing naked and I see him there. I am noticing myself on the ledge that runs right around our bathroom; it is a wooden ledge, and it separates the top half from the bottom half of the bathroom. I am noticing myself in the ledge, if that makes any sense, and mussing my hair a bit, and Johnny goes by mighty naked too and before I can whiz all out he's smiling at me and I'm mussing my hair up, real bad, and he just looks at me sort of curious, always curious, and I look back, he is noticing himself in my hair, and I notice myself in his chest, and we look and look and then I muss my hair some more and grin sheepish and he tilts his head and I grin faraway…

Johnny fixes an omelette and we eat it checking gleefully into each other's eyes. There is nothing wrong here, each is thinking. Nothing wrong in the least, in the world. There is chuckroast aplenty in our hearts. Chuckroast saignant, mon cheri. We rub each other down with the kindest words… It is time to "drop the beef." I do so and Johnny picks it up, and as he rises he brushes his nose across my flank and I shiver. The breakfast lasts and lasts…

. Johnny tells me stories and I hold his head gently in my lap, cooing into his ears. I tell Johnny a story and he rubs my forehead.

21

There is nothing wrong with the present situation. We are intelligent, vast people. We are endowed with capacities undreamt of by the city planners.

In the morning Johnny awakes sometimes before me, in which case I can see him staring and swaying or just tilting his head back and forth, and sometimes after me: I watch him sleep, puckered mouth, little drool. Sometimes I make-believe by putting my face right in front of his and slurping up the drool or just licking his lips, or just breathing onto his face and breathing in his breath—make-believe what I don't know, but it's make-believe. I love Johnny so much.

In the evening we see films from Austria, Sweden, postwar Hungary, Russia, and France. No Italian, we've decided. Among people we are polite and not easygoing. It becomes a question of adventurousness. I, for example, tend not to be quite adventurous enough, and Johnny gets bored and I get jealous—while Johnny recognizes that sometimes he's a trifle frivolous. We do not fault each other but instead fight viciously, with our hands and with books and with our feet, until we have finished the hate and can comfortably collapse into arms, each other's, indiscriminately, i.e. with true discrimination. "You see?" we would say to an onlooker. "We are real people too."

We eat, staring at each other's eyes, a little foggy, very happy, willing to die for each other.

MIGHTY FINE BABY FROM WHERE?

Gaston was born or given on a hot summer's day to a very drunk couple of "newly cauterized salamis." According to neighbors interviewed later, Mary and Joseph had recently had their "excess of pork" sealed up by the skin of a pig's small intestine, and suddenly Gaston was born. The circumstances were very mysterious, for neither Mary nor Joseph had noticed any of them.

Gaston, the son, was smart. He knew that Mary had often betrayed her Joseph, and that Joseph, dark with riff-raff pledging processed into a *kubbi* of nouveau assurance, had often betrayed his Mary and was moreover not to be thought much more than a vendor of hotcakes given a shot at some camels. (Ten years before: "Will *you* sell this camel?" "I shall, and will. And it will thus be made in twenty years that I shall purchase fifty." "Fifty, yea, and a thousand." A thousand, loud with the swill of dirt flaming, flight-owning honey-knuckle eyelids buckling, and rancid to the heart with gulp-loud and gulp-endless voyage, hardy with tunes to the center of class and provision, and sore with thoughts of burn-you-up lounge death—and moreover leafing as camels always do through their invisible bibles six feet high—a thousand camels he swore to own, and honestly speaking, he did get to own them, eventually. "Damn camels," Joseph would say several times.)

The first thing Gaston did after the birthing or appearance episode was catch Joseph's eye with a look that could curdle belief or rebellion. The first thing he said was "Honesty sparks God's joy."

At that, Joseph zombie rose to the height of his glaze and spoke loudly, well, and with love.

"I, Joseph, king of the stretches, with twice-blue apology holding myself like a grue guru, constantly poking at meats, I know, poking at ruckus-heady or sense-minded meats, meats, but nevertheless maintaining a certain dignity, do hereby announce to you, Mary, queen of my heads and rumps and of all my desert attainments, queen of forever, of each next and each moment of next, greeting the swallow with stacks of dulce, delicate sweetling—you, also, fighting the swarthy bar-nomads well, quite well, very fierce bitch— I announce to you that last weekend God came to me and opened my larval womb and swam to my birth and consolidated there some priciness, hard, hard priciness there, and Gaston, our Gaston, sits fused to the sitcom life of our forebears, giving it vast nobility thing...."

Of course it was a surprise to Mary that Joseph thought himself to have birthed Gaston, and this our icon eventually kicked him out of the house and encouraged him to roam far and wide over static and not-so-static realms of discovery, fear, and damnation. After six months' time she took the unusual baby and proferred him to some elders, who smoked and said "Yea" as if coming up with a very fine riff, and they made some plans, changed his name, and gave the baby some mighty fine drawers to spend the life of a holy man in, and by the time it came time to crucify him they were gone on safari.

An Account of the Respite

We enjoyed things pretty well that first year. Oh, we had our problems: the water leaked, the gas hissed, the kerchiefs tore in spots. The tissue was often soggy after showers, and in addition the hazelnuts were often bitter upon being opened. But these ills were as nothing compared with the joys we had. Our fiscal lives entailed these joys, we found. We found them often associated with car purchases and discotheque attendance and perfume selection. Purses often gave us joy, those with velour contours and shiny lambskin interiors, those with gold buckles and contoured shoulder-straps for the quiet, effective fit.

But our joy at times had noble causes. For example: the small red-brown-sorrel squirrel who after our passing was still a squirrel and not something else, for we had swerved to avoid it; this incident led to inward rejoicing. Other examples exist, abound. They led to our realization of our worth and the ultimate significance of ourselves in the world; this led, moreover, to our comprehension of the proud strength of everything and the likelihood that we were part of it, of this "cosmic plan," of this "grand design," of this "heaving destiny." We attended church.

Our church was pleasingly endowed and full of wealthy church-goers like Henry Mancini and Oscar de la Renta: it was a wealthy church and the liturgy rotated from Romance language to Romance language, missing however Catalan. At the end of the year we had a party. To the party we invited many and it was a highly successful affair. Henry Mancini sent his son, a charming fellow, to make presence.

Later things went quite sour. A baby was born and raised to its second year. It was a hale child with quiet brown eyes and a fairly thick tongue, nothing was immediately wrong, but then something was wrong, for it contracted a disease from a pig on an Amish farm we were visiting (our stay on the farm lasted several weeks and we adapted ourselves to their way of life) and died. We sued the Amish for negligence, which it had been, and left their environs without awaiting the end of the trial, which was tending in our favor: it had been a token move, this lawsuit, a way of showing the Amish they couldn't afford to be so sloppy forever.

This went on for quite a while and then we purchased a yacht and a house and a membership in a local boating club with which we became fed up quickly. The members were all men and women in their fifties, sixties, seventies, and eighties, not young like us. These turned out to be enthusiasts of the rolling bill, devotees of Mammon, pampered flesh. Gold, wool: for these they had tastes; they could not be trusted with Bach or the Etruscans.

We withdrew and enjoyed the surrounding "natives." This happened in the following way. In the first rush of being not in the boating club we had tried many things not many of which struck home, though some nearly did. We had fished, swum, rowed, motored, pedalled, scooped, and carved. Now. This latter had been done with a special knife purchased at the local "native"-run store, which was rustic. Thus.

We have gotten to know some of these "natives" quite well, though there is always a certain tension in the air. Still we talk and exchange "tall tales." Often we feel that we are patronizing these "natives" and that their affection is sham, their oscitance contrivance. Why, for example, do they refuse to discuss the tins they carry on their belts? This bothers us. They make good knives, however, and we buy them, Christmas gifts; this should be enough.

Soon we will go home. We believe that time will pass before the limit of tolerance is passed. In the meantime we observe and learn. But of course we will go home; then we shall see.

MANURE

He was six feet tall and every day pushed a wheelbarrow full of manure to the gardener's house. He smoked an old brand of cigarette. His hair was matted and huge. His workshirt was specked with animal and human matter and bore a now indecipherable logo.

He had many relatives. They mostly lived in the town and they came to see him at night in his room lit by one overhead bulb, floor, chairs, table all covered by the same red cloth. His uncle was his most frequent visitor and would spend hours berating him for his life. Three of his cousins, usually together, would come and speak with him about history and the future. Often they would bring sweets. He would remind them of their duties and describe the present exciting though frightening processes of change and growth as necessary and inevitable. They would speak about death. He would calm their worry by telling them the truth about death.

He had a lover, an older man with a passion for gardening and a very active involvement in the school. This man would speak to him about the need for him to express himself in a more consistent way. Speaking to his relatives was not enough, the man would say. He must learn an art and practice it. That way people across the world could know all that he knew. He would answer that that would not happen. People across the world would get tangled up. They would go to different boutiques for a week, or discuss things in a higher tone of voice for a day or two, and feel especially threatened around certain people, but they would not know anything that they didn't already. The man disagreed. The man suggested he was chicken. He answered that if he were chicken he *would* have an art and wouldn't speak to anyone close. It was much easier to be read in America than to have to be understood by one's relatives. It was only chickens, he said, that had to be known far away. One day he said that artists were just especially ambitious animals. Art was simply the human's mating call. Only the human that made the loudest, brightest call would get to reproduce. There was more than that kind of struggle, he said. His lover agreed that once.

One day he went to the market with his uncle, who wanted to make him buy some clothes. On the way he fell through a bridge and drowned. The river was very deep and his body did not float. It glided and bumped along the silty bottom for several days and arrived in a large city in the neighboring province, where it came to explain a murder that had taken place the week before. It was buried anonymously and his relatives never found out what had become of him. His uncle insisted that he had seen him swimming away at the point where the river bent out of sight, and since he was reliable everyone believed it was true. Only his cousins experienced any happiness, those next few weeks.

Ministry, eighth of September, 1911: The seven-head general is undergoing fractures—a loss of his hearing, misgivings in the hard afternoon, collapse of desire—and the legions are getting blamed. "Hell to be wended, warp and woof, throughout your lives! Septuagint be damned! Don't argue!" What can they do? They are many small men, unnoticed in the morning, weeping in the afternoon. They are as tiny as a half-baked clam.

"But maybe we have joy," one says. "Nah," replies his companion; "the commandantes took the projectors." "Then we must have the energy of young desire." "Yes," replies his companion, "but it is swallowed by the cruel meanings of his emperor's commands. Cruel meanings, swallowing our desire. Cruel." "Well I'll be damned," the first one says. "Yes," replies his companion.

The seven-head general urges on the legions. "Get." His bullhorn is spreading information at a huge rate, training his legions. "We understand the influence," they say. "We know what you say is true."

One of the legion, a hairy Jack, stands up and bellows to his friends, the other cohorts: "You are dim-witted and malignant. Every moment of your resting goes to hell on a fried horse. Your considerations are all as dreck for the tide. Do you know why? Do you know why?"

"No," the legion bellow as one, "no sirree."

"Well I'll tell you why," says the hairy Jack. "I'll tell you it's the weather. I'll tell you it's the political weather. The spiritual. Why, it's the intellectual weather."

"Then shouldn't we change it?" the legion bellows as one.

"Well of course you should change it," the hairy Jack bellows back. "Of course!"

But the weather changes and the legion retires to the huts, munching their fingers' knuckles, wondering about grain and the continuance of plenty.

INTERESTING EXHIBIT

It was a dark day in Cincinnati when the Consumer Throwbacks Exhibit opened in the Coliseum. Enormous fifties leftovers were hawking their glinting steel; pale sixties men were eating brisket by a very warm fire and sweating, sweating, till the droplets bounced off the tiles and into their plates, dissolving their food into bite-size Briskies. Near the door, a thirties woman, large yet unwholesome, was examining the facets of her opal, which was set in hand-shaped gold. (That far back, the charming guide informed us, you can't depend on clarity of any sort, any sort of understanding of living and buying—partly because these have gotten so different, partly because there is decay with the passage of Consumer Time. Many of us blanched and reeled before the size, the bulk, the tremendous alterations involved in the passage of something from this to that. Too large! we were thinking: Far too involved!)

There were others there, the mayor and his rival, and many small women with parasols trying to outdo the art nouveau facades. But we did not notice them! The man in the hat was a crouton! The women were geese in Nantucket! The mayor, the mayor of Cincinnati, was Alfred R. A gentle man, given to refusing the pleas of ill-saddled youths, given to quiet and contempt for the eery faces of plenty, preferring the majesty of the sit, the mayor was Alfred R.

We were so occupied! It was a dark day in Cincinnati, a day of thunder and gloom by the bushel, men arching backs like nobody's business, looking at clouds and seeing there all the things one can see, including the vastnesses of a mighty ocean liner's flank, the curlicues of the wake, the fish all bunched together and glowing in the plankton-ridden sea. The exhibit was launched by some scissors and hard by the entrance gate some boys launched a rocket, assassinating a crow.

An eighties girl in galoshes asked her mother for milk and her mother, a fifties woman, gave it to her in a rusticated blue glass, smiling, waiting for her daughter to drink, then tipping her head and pouring some more. The boys went in without tickets and launched into guffaws at the galoshes/milk exhibit, touching off stares of protest by all the people assembled at the cordon. But why were we here?

"Why are we here?" I heard a person ask. The person was young, fat, and extremely handsome. He was wearing a silk shirt with buttons and bore a look of atrocity revealed. "Why are we here?" He was a nineties man, free of the twentieth century, loved by the stars and the groups of stars and the holy order of those men who involve themselves in improving the lot of the multitudes ("multitudes" taken loosely as anything one cannot see the individual of or in or about, much like "masses" except with an essence of romanticism/ creedlessness, an abstractible word, lovely for itself and not the dozens of nations one will conceivably overrun—lovely not only for the people, I say: lovely for the sense it imparts to the brain as one says it, the alignment of synapse and breath in the purity of it, none of the mucosal grief of "masses"—for one thinks of the angels of Blake, not the suits and dishes of Lenin, who had dishes galore, but only the simple, which shows his totalitarianism was sincere).

The fat, handsome person was only poorly understanding things and had no way to know why the others were here. Cincinnati had reasons, the country had purposes—oh sure, love was rooting around in the peat, fantastic things were arising and spreading like desert grubs, noise was enormous—but we all remembered and we told the fat, handsome person what we knew about the modern world and the present situation of our nation, that this was a fine exhibit, important to behold, a way of life seldom understood in the world, cursed by the French, never seen by clumsy tribes, and for those of us not as fortunate as the fat, handsome man, a reminder of who we were, not quite ageless yet, not quite beyond the hold of meaningless dissection, not quite so fortunate as he, in his large silk shirt, not quite so clear about atrocity and the way things work, and as we told him so we noted with great emotion that there was no guilt or embarrassment on his face.

But that was only one day, and the exhibits were well maintained by the city of Cincinnati and the mayor and even by the women with parasols, who bunched together and assumed the poses of knowledge and contempt by the art nouveau facade of the great building, twirling, happy, refusing to participate, a great, urgent charm on their faces—and we, the multitudes endowed, threw ourselves into the thing and even invited our friends to the Coliseum, for when they could come.

Fire in the Crop

Home, election year.

There is a fire in the premium of our crop. Whippable Malicious has announced it fine over the system, revealing the proper devices in due but not jump-happy time. For that he is to receive a standard but not unpresented plaque.

The crop has been badly singed right where the President was due to eat, and the President and his arguable staff have been whisked to a fine desert location where the staff will engage in unpleasantries till dawn.

We have whipped that Malicious. Annoyed in travail at his own desire, wishing profound thoughts against the continued burn of the staple, bulwark of our simplicity, Malicious has gone about repenting the pleasures of his youth, annoying the symposia and causing the delicate rose of Mistress Bonaparte's bosom no end of roiling hatred. The Mistress Bonaparte, hardly happy in her cups and not to be amused by the petty rejectionist fever of a well-seated "scouring pad," has voted for that "scouring pad" to be whipped by men and pricked by clueless boys until he acknowledges the pleasures of his youth as divine eyes on adventure, all-revealing moments to be envied by every beautiful.

"I am encumbered!" he screams. "I am waylaid!"

Malicious? Were we discussing Malicious? While our crop is ravaged, the clocks are rewound, and the friends carouse with Hitler?

But that is a subplot.

But the subplot is not to be missed. Hitler has in fact arisen and Jenny has sat in on his bawlings for good minutes, veritable sections of hours, while Burden and Joff have assumed guises of mutual pursuit in order to attend. "We are segmentary animals," Hitler is screaming. "We have desires disjoint from our turmoils! Placeboes pertaining to phlegm! The rustic of cats!" And Jenny nods while Burden and Joff do hip-flicks and stomach-shimmies as they secretly bend their ears, dodging each other's darts as quickly as these can bounce, clever Burden, clever Joff, clever in their thirst for knowledge.

"Placebo!" Hitler bawls. "The ungulate memorize! The fecund 'isms' of my lunacy growl up the spiny decorum of the alma mater."

But Hitler? Were we discussing Adolf Hitler while the crop is ravaged, while the very moment of our glory shines in an untoward burst, a chemical proclamation of chemical decrepitude?

Well! May the dawning bring a charming arousal. For now there is nothing to be done. We will reckon on improvement and hope for new lust: we will underrate the opposition in order that our semblance be erased and our photograph enthroned. Our desires are disjoint from our turmoils! We are strength in others' confusion! And there is nothing to be missed.

Later, at night.
The fire has gone out and the President has returned triumphant. Malicious is dead and Hitler is about to explode. On the deep Asian front, changes are being wrought by many excited students.

MODERN WORLD PROBLEMS ACKNOWLEDGED BY US

3/15/88, Long Island
Great roiling bitterness in the Long Island society. Removing the back burners from public view. Madeleine, large, hopes against hope for the return of her husband. There are three horrible children living with her.

"Come down!" yells Malcolm to Betty. "The race of hate is over."

"Not yet!" yells Betty. "They're treating the eye."

Great bitterness in Long Island!

4/12/88
There was heaven on the ground, crawling around like a pig in the slop, the Irish observing, the Scots observing, everyone noticing heaven like a pig in the slop, a pig in the wet, crawling. A Scot spoke up: "Heaven is crawling much like an animal, toward the house I know so well."

"No," an Irishman said, "this is not June. Heaven does not crawl like an animal in December, only in June." But he was joking.

5/5/91
Attorneys were quieting the lands of excitement, the great fiery hordes and the spunk, the spunk of the many.

"Accuse me wrongly, Malcolm."

"I cannot, Betty."

"You must, Malcolm. It's the only way."

"Well, Betty—but I shan't enjoy it."

"No need for that, my Malcolm, my sweet."

4/14/80

Here in the forest, great, fantastic, luminous forest, beast of all our cares, horny devil for the winnowing, we sat and fostered our magnificence. It was tiring eventually and some of us set out for snacks: Harvey, June, Alfred and Irene. Alfred and Irene found only the Workingmen's Club and Harvey and June found only the stadium. In both there were snacks galore, but none of them thought to look inside, and none of them had money anyhow.

Then I set out and found a great mountain of snacks, which I brought back by mule and set in front of my dear associates. "Perhaps," I said, "we will never be hungry again." "Fat chance," they seemed to be saying as they ate. "Roiling fat chance of that."

Here in the forest we had us a great understanding of largeness, and when the apocalypse dove in for a chat we were ready, explaining the mercies, describing the avant-garde in high, high terms full of light and desire, and the apocalypse seemed impressed and went to pester some others, youngish beauties by the river, and when it discovered we were also those beauties the apocalypse went away for a good long time and we were allowed to strive for betterment and even Messiah.

4/14/1789

There was something seriously wrong with the upper atmosphere. In the topmost reaches, those which are way beyond the range of even our most exciting equipment, strange things were brewing, great insubstantial vatfuls of awful hybrids, terrible combinations of inorganic and, yes, organic. And most of us did not know what to do, being on the ground in Central America, a difficult place in any condition, so we merely continued to stare or absolve or lubricate according to our station.

Later certain people arrived with equipment that could speak more accurately to the situation in the upper atmosphere, but other terrible things began happening and we felt very lost, there in the jungles of Central America, very lost indeed, and no one to complain to.

Regarding the Uncustomary Events of 1989 Which Occurred Here and There Around Northern Europe

Oct. 31

Between myself and the president's ring of associates lies a barren plain. Across the plain I send certain winged messengers with messages of determination and well-wishing-within-bounds. The president walks over and hands me a note he has scratched out in his blood: "TO THINE OWN SELF BE TRUE." I examine this message several times over before raising my left arm, which I have kept sleek and attractive, and whistling with my well-formed lips. At this my friends charge whistling and waving at the president, who is only one quarter of the way across the plain. They bear placards (I cannot read them from behind). The president wails a long, powerful wail at the sky and simultaneously his men, helpless across the plain, watch him be assaulted unto death.

Nov. 2

Some men of the crazier sort were lounging around on the plain hard by the plain of the president (as it came to be referred to in the disgusting shorthand of the energetic, bustling masses). These other men were hitting each other upon the nose with their fists, bumbling around with a mix of niceties and criminal exaltations in their heads, feeling required to hit, hit, hit again and again until the blood might ooze and the angry protectors of liberty might arrive to quell the disturbance and put the craziest of the men in jail. The jail was not located here. The jail was a sunspot called Magnafora, which means Large Forums, for its surface mottled in squares.

Twenty days were whiled away! in that sunspot. The men grew hotter and hotter and regretted ever more the hitting of the other men. But what could be done? They were in a sunspot, enormously far from earth, impossibly hot, too hot to visit, quite mottled in squares that cataclysmically burped each other's edges several times each day, o horrible place—and what does one do with some criminals in a sunspot? You tell me!

Nov. 11

The president has recuperated from his violent death by opening dialogues with the worlds of the ancient Irish. The residents thereof deplore his relentless incursions but understand and even respect his motives. (That is one of their strengths, that uncanny, quintessentially Irish ability to push through the veils of pique and see the nudnick for his goals.) The president now has life and returns to the plain, where his assailants (my friends and I) have disappeared and are searching the hinterlands for a touch of nutmeg. Will we find it? Will the president catch us first?

Nov. 21

Right by the plains, the plain of the president and the plain wherein the crazier men hit each other, it turns out there's a pond. It has fish like endless gewgaws. A man in dungarees sits forever on a bank casting and reeling, casting and reeling, repeating to himself the Elder Edda endlessly, hoping for some clue as to its meaning, for there is hardly any epic of the Northern Europeans he has not mastered in all its subtleties. The president pokes through a shrub, hoping not to disturb the dungareed man. The dungareed man is not disturbed. The president asks for a fish or a bottle of water. Several times the president asks for these things. Finally the dungareed man suspects foul play and radios his humane society chairman. That man arrives in spats and examines the president, who lies face down in the mud and tries not to move.

The dungareed man knows that I am nearby with my friends, searching for nutmeg. It is only out of the goodness of his heart that he has called the humane society instead of unleashing on us the president's rage.

Dec. 13 (Friday)

It is hard to imagine, but the crazy criminals are out of the sunspot and have been for thirteen, eight, twenty-one days. The president found me and buried me alive for a few days, but I resisted by calling upon the Teutonic Rivals, who are stronger than the worlds of the ancient Irish and can banish most anything. The sunspot is weeping at noon for its lost charges, who, we are assured by the Academy, were starting to like it there. At the pond, the dungareed man and I fish, horribly, endlessly, eighteen, nine, twenty-eight days at a stretch, upon which I must get up for rushing about. I marvel at his endurance and often feel his muscles, just in case the answer is obvious. It is not. The fish we catch are regrettable, horrible, mean.

Great Sea Occurrence

The life of sea is quite something, whales, shoals of fish, enormous stretches of sheer blank nothing. So one gets to thinking, and somewhere in there one thinks of God, that other, and why He exists and where. Why does He allow ships to founder, is one of the "how" questions. One can't answer "how." So one plots one's course, fierce little ship, along the barren stretches of the roiling ocean. Roiling and barren, and also bleak.

What is there to do? Matthew and I play cards, and sometimes we play for hardtack, and usually Matthew wins, but I am so happy to be envisaging the future (for that is what we talk about together, the future) that I don't mind at all. Who likes hardtack anyhow, and what sort of major problems is our ship going to have that we'll actually have to eat it?

I have other friends on board, John and Saul and others.

This particular story is about one voyage we all took that proved to be quite disastrous. We were sailing the huge blank nothing as always, eyes piercing fog, hardtack changing hands, and out of the fog appeared a bank of something. Well, we weren't near land so our one-oak monkey decided it was a ship and yelled out that here was a ship astern or wherever it was and that did it, the ship was all eyes and started turning toward us and then boom! Well, that didn't make any sense, of course, so the lot of us started wondering what was going on that this ship was firing on us so we yelled out some things we perhaps shouldn't have and we also fired on it, once. Then it yelled back that we'd better not fire on it anymore. Then we yelled that it had fired on us, and we suggested a general ceasing of fire, not touching, not firing, going each our separate way, in opposite ways, and the other ship yelled back that it agreed, so we angled our ships just right. Well we were nearly maneuvered all right and we happened to get almost flush with the ship, it going backward, when suddenly boom! But this time, boom boom! And many more, and this was foul, we thought, and we sank, and many drowned but I and Matthew and John and Saul were saved and we had to downright scramble over to the other ship which picked us up in a markedly desultory way and sat us down and dried us off and gave us some vittles and each a bundle of hardtack.

Now sitting on deck each with a bundle of hardtack, here on this new deck, we each got to wondering and finally we stopped a well-hatted man in silk and asked him why this ship had sunk ours. "This is the ship," he said, "the ship of the ocean. This is the only ship."

Of course we were stunned. Naturally. We stopped someone else, with an even better hat and even finer silk. "This is the goddam ship," he said, and we decided to wait for someone else.

"This is the ship," a very simple young man finally told us. "On it we live and wait. It is the only ship. The only ship on the ocean. Others, yes, are plying the ocean with sterns of oak and prows—who knows?—of baleen…But the real ship—do you know ship? The power in it? Every ship has its crew, but what is truly ship? The ship of the deepest moment of ship?"

All right, we thought, all right, we'll play along, this is the one true ship, we'll say, we'll say it a lot, so we said it a lot, this is the ship, how bizarre we were thinking, to think such a thing, but we said it right, we enjoyed some times on this ship, the ship, but all along we were thinking, and the food was quite bad after that, mostly rice, and we kept on saying yes, this is the ship, oh yes, how bad we were thinking, how really bad to own the seas, and after a while I kept to myself while the others were shown the prow and the poop and the iron-ribbed sides, strong ship, until finally I got disgusted and after we had sunk five more ships and slowing was not in the cards, it seemed, I decided to take things into my own two hands and I pulled the plug, the big brown plug amidships, and there we sank, and though I might die, I was thinking, at least the five more ships we'd soon sink will not die, how absurd it would be for five more ships to die, the sea is so big and I miss my home, how strange to be sinking ships so far from home.

Glug, glug, glug, glug, glug.

But I was smart, I pulled the plug right next to the sixth ship, and as soon as they realized it was all up with us they helped us onto their deck and dried us off and said tsk tsk tsk and arrested our captain and the rest of our time on that ship we swabbed the black deck till it shone with such black, and we polished the little black fixtures on all the black cannon, and that's how they put us to work for millenia, polishing black, until finally, at the end of one year, they dropped us in Italy, where we scampered and gambolled back to our homes and our big fat mothers all dressed in black and ate the biggest old dishes of everything fine and never thought of hardtack again, and thought about God all the time, and our thought made more sense, and we ate and were happy and that was quite the end of all that.

STILL LIFE WITH DISASTER (U.S.)

THE CAT-WOMAN CLAWS, RED-CAPED AND SENSUOUS, CLAWS CLAWS CLAWS AT THE SKYSCRAPER. SLOWLY HER LIPS BARE ELLIPTICAL MOON OF TEETH, THE MOON ARCS LEFT TO RIGHT, RIGHT TO LEFT, SLOWER, RESTS IN CENTER, HER HEAD TURNS, SHE FACES US. THERE IS NOTHING, HER FACE SEEMS SUPERIMPOSED ON A TATTERED LAMPSHADE, WE CAN ONLY IMAGINE WHAT IS LEFT SILENT IN THE DEPTH OF HER FOLDS. HER HEAD TURNS BACK SLOWLY, SLOWLY, BACK TO THE SKYSCRAPER, HER LIMBS ARE MOVING ALMOST IMPERCEPTIBLY, THEN SHE SHIFTS AND CLAWS AGAIN, CLAWS CLAWS CLAWS, SLOWLY, SHE IS THE CAT-WOMAN.

Mary swivels by the coffee machine her arms a galleon of tuck-and-wave proofs, and stops. She tilts a lazy head and stops. Suddenly she stops in her tracks and her head sticks out, she is listening.

"Oh gum," she says to Chip as she stops, "this is spooky, Chip. There's a clawing coming from this wall. I swear."

Chip stops and comes over. He hears the clawing as he stops. "Damn. This is a nice place, a really nice place, but then this clawing, it's like a nightmare but you can't wake up even when you stop breathing, I'm barely breathing (because I hate it so much when something hideous like this happens, I mean what could that be, it could be anything), what is it? What do you think it might be, Mary? What do you judge?"

"God, I don't know. It could be anything, Chip. Hey, Mr. Hubert! There's a clawing coming from this wall, Chip heard it too. It could be anything. What do you think it is?"

Jon stops, rotund. "I don't know," he bellows, "I haven't *heard* it." He starts to walk on.

"Please stop," Chip says. "We're kind of freaked out, this kind of thing doesn't happen in regular life, couldn't you just stop here for a minute like we have and listen please?"

Jon stops and tilts his head. In the relative silence he hears a clawing. A gasp escapes his throat. He lifts an arm and waves it frantically behind his back. "Mr. Brass! Mr. Brass! There's a thing here, there's a weird thing going on. Mr. Brass?" Jon stops and turns around just in time to catch a view of Huck Brass coming out of his office.

Mary announces the discovery. "We've found a clawing, Huck! There's a lot of clawing going on."

Huck arrives and tilts his head, holding up an arm to dim the hubbub. "My God, you're right, Ms. Seminal, you're right indeed. There is a veritable clawing going on here."

Bunko and Killer and Swine pass by and stop. "Well then there now. What's this here going on here?" No one notices them and they tilt their heads.

Randy calls out from the hallway, "Is someone hurt? Should I get something on my way out?"

"It's clawing!" He stops but everyone is suddenly gabbing.

"Quiet?" Someone hears him and nudges the rest to silence. He listens. "Okay," he says, "Mary, Mr. Norse, Brass, Jon-Jon, Messrs. Grunnheck, we've got a weird situation on our hands here, friends, we're swooping in the mad endeavor now, we're swivelling on righteousness over monkey-tunes, let's not screw, let's not do boners, we're heavy on this one, ladies and gentlemen, we've got to be a little bit heavy with this, let's see, let's see, let's see."

Huck steps up then and puts an arm on Randy's shoulder. "Randy, I think we just need to stay calm, is all. I think if we just weather this like we've weathered the other disturbances in our office, I think if we just do that it's going to be just fine. I don't think there's anything to worry about. I think we've got angels in our desks and that's all we need." (Mock-conspiratorial wink to Chip.) "Now nobody panic, okay? Okay okay?"

Jon steps to the fore and takes off his jacket. "I've got the say on this, Mr. Brass. This is the simple outcome: We are going to lay low and find a television. I have a feeling this is something serious. Everyone stay put."

"Well yes," Mary says, "but we don't have a television. Why don't we just all have coffee?" Everyone agrees provisionally and the discussion goes on for four more minutes and thirty-six more seconds.

THE CAT-WOMAN TIRES AND SAGS. SHE TURNS ON A TELEVISION AND WATCHES SOME CEREMONIES. SUDDENLY A MAN IS KILLED, IT IS A CAT-WOMAN IN SEOUL WHO HAS TIRED AND EXPLODED A GYMNASIUM, THESE THINGS ARE HAPPENING SAYS THE ANNOUNCER, BEWARE, THE CAT-WOMAN PULLS OUT SOME EXPLOSIVES AND TIES THEM TO THE SKYSCRAPER. SHE TURNS AND LOOKS AT THE STREET, HER EYES LOST IN THE IDIOTIC PLAINS OF HER FACE, HER LIPS SAGGING TOO MUCH NOW, THE TEETH TOO PROMINENT....HER CARRIAGE SAGS MORE AS SHE WATCHES THE PEOPLE STUMBLING ABOUT AND SHE HAS TO ACTUALLY PULL HERSELF AROUND TOWARD THE SKYSCRAPER....IT RAINS. THE CAT-WOMAN SHIFTS HER EYES TO THE EXPLOSIVES AND EVERY MUSCLE IN HER BODY TENSES IN RAW ANTICIPATION.

THE DUMP-MAN

How wonderful: the dump-man has it in for me. I sit up late with energy, with Kool-aid, with virulent strains of the impossible lacing my head, my head like a Roman's with its beak and mop. The dump-man has it in for me. Ask me once, I tell you: strange. A strange design upon our house. A shew of monsters. A cudgelling of props, a flight of migrant fancy to the corer of our bones: "Halloo pack poonies! Doncha lead them poonies out the private drive, we beat yore bee-hinds bad!" The corer of our bones is one stark dude. He and the dump-man have it in for me. Forgetfulness on rampage, Mathilda with her seven sons, all seven, leaves kitty litter in the kitchen. Boys don't poop in sand, Mathilda! She once had cats aplenty. She is pro-tecting me, in her own fluffed perennial way, from the dump-man and the corer of our bones. She has a fierce maternal presence, she staggers the matriarchs, she is power-love on wheels. (You can see it in the way she stands.) She and Hans, brilliant Hans, Hans of the emoluments, ballet Hans, Hans upon a dime, protect me from my fate, they are so fateless, and from the dump-man and the corer of our bones.

With anger on the uprise though, and beauty clamming up, and all the various percentages one has to deal with, it seems unlikely I will win. The dump-man will unnerve the masters, settle it with Hans, achieve Mathilda with her seven rumps, and charge full head into the cup of my irony, my pure, gentle irony, which doesn't smell of the academic. And that corer, that corer of our bones, he'll beat my behind terribly, excruciatingly. Hans and Mathilda will live out their lives in idle desperation by a sluggish lake or maybe in a city or both, and I will be as nothing, a dumped bag of coreless bones. That is the way it is with this sort of thing.

OONCHI HAS A BAD DAY

Oonchi goes hauling ass across the rock-strewn expanse of dead Farmer Ferd's land. He is simply hauling ass, a white supremacist, baldly powered by his sausage-white legs and baldly engaged with his forearms and hands, strong the forces they emblematize for him in his balding white head so full of ideas. That is Oonchi, engaged to his hands, hauling bouncy ass across the rocky place, a white supremacist in dust tracks, puddly tracks in later rains, puddle-puddle dust tracks.

Now he is paused, holding a form in an arch, the form of one waiting, in an arch, an American arch of cement and plaster, on Farmer Ferd's land. The air is criss-crossed by faint black and white birds in a huge holding pattern in front of the arch, and Oonchi has to hold himself still to keep from doing something, though there really isn't anything he could do right now, and the arch can just support the pressure of his forearms and hands struggling in a certain way to keep Oonchi from doing something right now.

Oonchi starts thinking to himself I've got to let go, I've got to let go, let go of all my problems, just let go of them all, I've just got to let them away right now, there's just nothing I can do right now for these problems of mine, I've got to let them go, I've got to let go of my problems—I've just got to let go of my problems, I'm to the point here of disbelief, the point, letting go, let go problems, I'm hardly believing it, let go, let go he thinks to himself as he grips the arch seeing in his mind a wall he could climb and over it his family tree in which he played but fell once and then ate candy.

If you've ever dusted a house top to bottom for an hour longer than it took to dust it, or even maybe two hours, dusted the chairs made of plastic that didn't need to be dusted much and also the window and the fire escape handle on the window and then dusted what else there was to dust, including jokingly the cat, jokingly your face, and then dusted another minute the television before turning it on and dusting some more and then dusted the other television and then turned it on too and then dusted perhaps the pornography before opening it and then throwing at it a dart, a heavy dart in a sex-murder scandal, and then dusted again jokingly the cat thinking "kick"—then you've been crazy too and you know why Oonchi was heaving his weight against the old American arch on Farmer Ferd's land, thinking a lot about his forearms and shit, and you could have been a white supremacist too as a solution to your problems, but instead you've discovered poetry, also probably even a way to express it, a bit and a bit, which is better than murdering people and leaning up against arches, and you're doing okay.

Oh, and if you're like me and you've never dusted a house like that or something as big as a house like that you're probably not crazy enough to become a white supremacist even under pressure so don't worry about it, and if you've discovered poetry all the same don't worry about not being crazy because even poets are better off not crazy and certainly it's not good to think you might conceivably have turned out all different under different circumstances, for people are better off not thinking that about themselves and it's what you have to think if you're crazy and you're better off this different way, you really are.

In any case none of us is Oonchi but he's leaning up against an arch kind of wishing he didn't have so many problems but he really does, he's got lots of problems right now, and he doesn't know if it's him or his lungs that are causing him to think back so hard on everything including his problems but he feels a little weak about the whole thing and he's not thinking very straight or anything and what he does is he starts banging his head against the arch and wishing it weren't so strong an arch but this is it, this is really it, and he stops wishing the arch weren't so strong, he just wishes he weren't so bloody but there it is, and he stumbles back to town and down the main street and goes to the cops and lies down on the bench of the cops and then he starts moaning and it's all about the black guy with a rod and no shirt and after some time a woman wets a rag and wipes his head clean of blood and dust and plaster flakes and the people convene in a soothing buzz of ambition and Oonchi turns over to face a wall which conveniently lunges at him and wraps around him into a well-bricked gritty sleep full of handicapped children.

MEMORIES OF STATES 1938
(LAUNCH, EPIPHANY, SPHINCTER)

My earliest recollection is of a washboard in Missouri and a large Asian man doing his shoes on it. I don't believe a thing my mother told me about my past, like that the washboard couldn't have happened. I also remember the man screwing in a template; maybe he's tired. My mother said it was ridiculous. (Missouri is a state for wonder, it grows on you as you get to know it. It's somewhere in the Midwest, I know that, the Midwest of this country, and lots of people move there from the outer states. If you look at books about it you'll have no idea.)

I'm going out with Pucky, a gentle soul from Kansas. She admires my shoes, which pleases me no end because they're from Illinois, the state of my father's birth. Pucky tells me I wear them akimbo. I show her akimbo and she laughs mouth open; she knows what she means.

We're going to the Arkansas. I say "the" because that's how my uncle says it, that's where he's from. Pucky picks the motels and loads the car; I feed the dogs. I'm slothful to the point where Pucky says she's in masochism with me.

I admire her turn of mind.

When I was twenty I sought a guru for my spiritual pain but there wasn't any, no pain and no guru. It was kind of weird to realize all that, I still remember and I remember only important things, which Pucky says is stupid. "That's stupid," she said when I told her. Anyhow, in no pain I sought a guru and now I realize I just need someone to know, like Pucky.

We're starting for the Arkansas!

Pucky likes South Carolina a lot. She says it makes her tingle. She tells me about the Gaster book in which the Carolinas unite over cold roast and parsnips, even though I've read it twice with a headache.

We stop for lunch in a little town in Georgia, it's kind of ugly in all the sun but the food is reasonable and reminds me of a dinner at three with largish feting relatives at ease. We admire the waitresses in velveteen and the schoolchildren in full romp. Pucky nudges my elbow and stares into my eyes, not really vacantly but she's definitely somewhere else. I grin.

The car doesn't start. I zone out on the local paper, admiring the bingo-club feel, the luncheons and parties and quotes that evoke for me a certain childhood, not mine but very intense. The mechanic takes forever but doesn't really overcharge; he insists I keep my change. We drive!

Alabama treats us to a real show. In one city are the Dancing Elite, a group of "headstrong but lithe" young women who breeze about to classical music, occasionally contorting in ways that recall to one one's sadism. In one town we encounter "races of speed," which are triathlons featuring splendid young men in green and red. Finally, right on the splendid border, by a deep and fragrant lake, hundreds of youths dive from rocks, splitting our heads with their manifold hubbub.

In-between the car nearly explodes and we find a nice mechanic for not too much money.

The upshot of our Mississippi experience is unfortunately small, almost insignificant. Mississippi in our eyes comprises a poverty-absorbed territory and a good fistful of muddy waters, unprofitable except to Pucky's generous sponge of an imagination: she thinks of crocodiles and worms. Exactly that, in fact, is the upshot: and it takes us two days.

Later suddenly I develop a rare case of ankle swelling and Pucky pretends not to notice. I limp and swear and we argue like demons for hours but then suddenly she's in my position, driving the car, adoring the sights I won't notice, experiencing the driving need of dual solitude. We enter the Arkansas, examine what we've come for, experience the values, and leave. Mississippi is again a cruel disappointment. Alabama grants us joy in the form of troupes and then in Georgia we visit the birthplace of (a) a President, and (b) a famous composer of music. South Carolina turns my stomach and overjoys Pucky; and home I am full of memories, despite mother.

Hallelujah. The land of our fathers is still a major voyage.

WE MANAGED TO DO QUITE A BIT

How many of us were there really, lounging in the quad? Hubert was gone, had to run the office. The office was large but not as large as the quad, and needed the expertise. The quad was remarkable, and there were many of us in it. A few of us were organizing resistance. The rest of us were trying to entice passers-through. There was nothing extraordinary about our efforts in that direction, though we succeeded in nearly a dozen cases.

"How do you run this thing?" First we had to make coffee; then, the visitor plied and running, we explained some ins and outs. "The maniple is the smallest unit and is just enough men to run a situation. The squadron is next, consists of seven maniples, and is just enough men to keep the situation going in all its branchings. Next the battalion, seven squadrons, and with that we come to the top level of order. The battalion general is less powerful on the individual level than is the maniple head, but much more so when it comes to influencing men of power and strength."

The timberline got lower and jungle started spreading again, to cities and other inhabited places. At first the jungle business turned out to be public relations; we had to find a way to convince the people involved. Some of them disliked the animals of the jungle, animals we see sewn onto scarves and book sacks. Some of them were ready to roll with the mention of lilacs, which bear a harmful poison. Others were merely petulant. We took care of that. No one minded, then, much later, when we altered the sea.

The sea is a museum. It houses some of the rarest creatures and some of the most astounding scapes. The moon regulates the top .0000024 percent of its motion and engages wanderers in creation. Creation of sea! For the sea is more than what meets the eye, and less. The sea is a museum.

It was a matter of calculating fluency. People were not fluent, cities were not fluent, but the ocean was fluent. The moon could not be trusted; enticements abounded for such activities as astronomy, merchandising, marketing. Even construction work had its adherents. The sea was there, alone, large, tumescent with the giggles of centuries. Only the door remained to be built, and we built it.

Around that time we were audited, were asked many questions, some of which we could answer, many of which we could not but didn't have to, and one that we couldn't but had to, and that one's a stumper. It's about a day in spring, thick with discourse and large flying thoughts of attainment, attachments rustling as they hung from our belts, a day for effort and explanation, a sort of military day. We were in the quad that day, lounging as it were, trying to keep the joy silent. How many? Too many, perhaps. But why must we know, if we only admit there were many?

The method of distillery was remarkable but we angled down from that "sphere," or "angled attention area," to the better place of "spheres," or "unangled distraction void." For in "sphere" there were ugly women and men of terrible pallor quoting Brandisi and Volk, Harding and Lancaster, and they altogether stank of disrespect for the Absolute so it was "spheres" for me, that generally more nebulous region where one speaks of the young men on stilts as "they who remain."

The physical descriptions will suffice: of what? We remained in that place, longing for better, not quite knowing what we had, until we were vanquished by *sheer unintelligible goodness* and had to give up our vain questing and settle uninhibited in the rocky place, with many menservants and maidservants to boot, an altogether attractive deal which pinned the new moniker upon us: "virtuous."

We were only virtuous to those others because we would occasionally spin down from the underbelly of chaos and display our new "wares" to the inept.

In any case it was a remarkably pure situation for us and our type and we lost ourselves there in the ruins, beseeching the pitiful to reveal their smarm, having a grand old time with the broken means of identification, altogether *losing ourselves*.

Enough about us! Tell us about you! It is high, high time you spoke of that warm fuzz, that unyielding zoom, that crackpot to-do, and that one old thing, that one disastrous porcelain you've always wanted to break....Break it! But tell us about it first and don't just sit there, *do it!*

HOME FAT PLOT

"It's so absurd, really. Here's Amy saying she wants me to come to North Carolina and spend hours and days with her, and then she says she wants to find another lover."

This had happened before and now she was angry. I tried to console her. "It's boring."

"I know. Now Cathy was supposed to take care of the place while we were gone, but the kids were there, and they belly-crawled over to the TV where War Games was one hell of a bright image."

"Yes, I know. And then she says, 'I'm going to mess up your pretty new car and see what the hell you think of no transportation.' Bundle her up and throw her out, you know?" We exchanged conspiratorial glances, which was in fact because we knew what we were talking about.

"Yes. Let's maybe stop gossiping; it's acceptable only when there is no possibility of a third party being privy to the messages. Have you noticed the quote marks?"

"Yes." I brushed a fly from my nose (it had in fact alighted there) and took the phone. "Hello?"

"Hello. Which number did I dial? Was it 623-9684?"

"I don't know. I presume. Some would discount the whole thing as a trick of the imagination, your imagination—but I am far kinder. Don't worry about a thing when you call me, even if I'm the wrong number, the wrong sound, the wrong thing altogether; don't fret at anything to do with me: I am yours, in a very real sense, and you should remember it. There is a wind blowing through the universe right now, and it is me. Your universe, me the wind. Let us rejoice. And when...Hello?"

"Would you mind paying attention to me now?"

I couldn't believe the rudeness! She was buxom, enormous. "Hello, my buxom, enormous darling. I am yours."

"So Amy would really get mad at the whole thing, she would just shove up all that was happening into a tiny screech of nothing at all, literally nothing at all. And I would sit, all alone with my frets, my happiness, just everything blowing through the air at any moment, taken at random. And things would start rolling."

"But where would you start? I am here; the phone is there; existence looms large on the outside of all that—phone, me." We shifted our weight (buttocks) on the cold gray bench that had for a long time been our sole means of support. "And there is a difference, my love, between tears and piss. Nor can they be discharged simultaneously." My head rested in the crook of her knee and we fell into a gentle hum for a few minutes as the light flickered in the violent storm (electric) that was raging out-of-doors. How the gentle hum? How from tirade of macho ebullition to the gentle sea (rocking doves, swirling lighthouses) conveyed to the reader by means of the phrase "We fell into a gentle hum"? How the end, how the beginning? Where the punch and plot?

THE ZOOLOGIST

First, a vision of a man, fairly lonely, lost as it were in a great sea of mischief. A man, certainly, but what kind of man? A lonely man, lost in the mischief of others, mischief wrought indiscriminately by others. The others, how are they? They are either good or bad, nice or not nice, intelligent or stupid, wise or boorish. Some are refined, this is certain, and some have expensive tastes. Others are content with the simplest effects. They are simply others; no elaboration is required.

Titmouse of Arabia. Flinging wrasse. These names and others have been the man's life. They have risen out of dust and created him, marvelling much at his contours, his inhibitions and desires. Shucking fairy-dove. Maltese kite.

Connecting one thing with the next, the next, the man has established, in his head, the connectedness of all things. He has taken one thing, a wren perhaps, in one hand; he has assumed the position of arbiter with the rest of the things, which include buffalo; he has, as arbiter, then chosen; the chosen, say a buffalo, has stepped forward; the man has compelled. The buffalo, compelled, has lain quiet; the man has observed; the man has then taken, slowly, the buffalo, the buffalo, into his other hand. Wren, buffalo. These things have been related. Proceeding thus, there has been truth.

Glaucous evening wren. Nut-and-coffee buffalo. He has been reading. In his mind there are distinctions. The life he has led has led him to distinguish, and the nut of it is, he has been reading.

He has been reading of lights and shoots, of the twisting demanded of a dying eel. In the depths of these books have been souls, perfect little paper souls with angry little fingers, fluttering eyelashes, the gentlest of lips. The man has been oblivious. To him it has all been very interesting.

These books he has been reading: they have yellowed him to life, the phenomenon of life. They have put paid to any notions of what it is, life, and have extended his mind beyond the tracks of an erstwhile train. They have caused him to think, and, thinking, he has uncovered paths through the brush. One such path: Life: life, life a collection, a collection of pairs, of randomly ordered pairs of conveniences. These, these pairs: assembled into a whole, a randomly ordered whole, a constellation, a monastery of forces. These forces his blood; this blood his whole, *the* whole: a monastery of pairs.

This path ends with a salute to adventure, the great organizer. And he is still.

He is tall and has a moustache. His hat sits atilt atop his head. He reads in his library, which is forested with books. He read with an accent, a faraway lilt recalling tinsel and girls.

His habits are few and far between. There is a world between his loves and his needs. Thus he finds hours in which to read and read; read he does, incessantly. He is a zoologist.

Zoology is a far science, and there are souls in his books.

• • •

This morning, a walk in the country. Fleeing buff-goose. Overhead and underfoot, the wonders of a lifetime, great beneficent lifetime.

There are questions that have stayed with the man for years, tugging at the sleeve, ruining milkiest firelight. There are drooping eyelids, two of these, and they inhabit the swamplands of his face. There are other things. There are color, shape, the beauty of sly thighs. Triangle-maned bear moose. There are memories, thoughtless fastenings-on. There are dreams; these occur at night. (Mixing and mixing, the elders stir a potion of paralyzing gas that fastens down your left arm to stimulate the right. Robed and manicured men of ninety-five wander among the numina and report back their tales. They tell of cardboard men in nightshirts, of pathways that swirl and fall, often with force, on our radios, our beds, our wives. These men are the elders of loads, dray-horses of the spirit.

(The elders cough and cough: "Damage has been done. A thorough revamping of well-nigh everything is in order. This meeting has begun." But ho! they retire. They retire to their villas by the sea. Awaiting them are iridescent wives in scarlet and green, holding firstborn by their bulbous heads. The waves lap the sand nicely, like tired, abstracted ladies.

(The zoologist is on the beach, hiding, grabbing spare seconds to gaze at the glowing fish, the like of which he has amazingly never seen.)

Shh! The zoologist is dreaming.

• • •

Taras Bulba lip-skunk. The zoologist knows it lives its life deep in the forest, deeper even than the triangle-maned bear moose. Now he listens for the first time, and it tells of its loves among the trees, loves with other animals, loves with other skunks. His face turns soft, his eyes droop lower into his face, he takes the skunk into his hand and caresses its body, its back and tail. As arbiter, the man chooses from among the masses of beasts; he finds a ferret. Having compelled, the man begins to grasp; the ferret slowly, slowly is taken into his other hand. Skunk. Ferret. Ferret. Skunk. These things are related. The proceedings have yielded truth.

The man sits alone in his library, which is forested with books. He is holding a rag which has been wrung of drops. It is placed slowly, precisely over the dainty-tongued mouth of the Taras Bulba lip-skunk. The lip-skunk breathes, the skunk's chest heaves, the animal dies. The proceedings have yielded death.

A song from oblivion in a dead voice, deep and cracked, issues from within the long old chest:

> "I want to sing a merry, merry lie,
>   to spy, and spying die.
> I want to live a murdering show,
>   to kill, and killing know;
> A bookcase can commit no sin.
>   Come, o day: begin."

Goodnight.

THE BAD THING

Heinrich is dead meat. Slamming shut his grandmother's door, he faces the squadron with a look that equals murder. Fast unraveling of the obvious, and: "Penniless heavers of all depth-undoing, unlaureled toadies of Satan, cook me in your headiest stew, go ahead." The squadron nudge and giggle. Here they come.

First they dismember Heinrich. One limb from the next, each from the major case, every protruberance finds its rest on one of grandmother's china treasures. "Heinrich? Could you bring me a tisane?"

First it is the leader, pensively poking the varicose. Then the others enter, whispering now delight, now courage, now hatred for the people. Grandmother is placed, part for part, in the blue-glass goblets she's been saving for a reunion of the members of her clubs. She is energetically shoved this way and that to make room for the stampede of the opponents.

The opponents enter big-time. There is a major fight but no one is hurt save Adolfo, a smallish youth from Cincinnati, who loses his fingers. Then there is a toast of goblets and a clicking of china. The stew is rendered more wholesome with cupfuls of oregano and parsley. The leader of the non-opponents congratulates Adolfo, rattling his cage though with a somber word of wisdom: "Never stand secure in the limelight. The virtue of our ranks is in their subjugation. Don't fry your lust in the butter of your solitude either. Just take care of those stumps."

71

CITY STORY

The man was holding on to a spade with his left hand, this was true.

There was nothing else unusual about the man, but he had very large muscles.

Very large muscles, fibrous and lovely, and a difficulty with words, but that wasn't visible.

He certainly was holding a spade.

The woman became his mistress over a period of a few days. First they kissed, then they were lovers for maybe a day, day and a half, then everyone called her his mistress, that's how it happened.

Sometimes in the inner city you can't tell just what what is.

She was poor, rather unlovely, but given to a wildness you wouldn't expect out of anyone, and the man fell in love, rather fast, so fast they were lovers right away, and then she was his mistress.

She was his mistress in the way that two men on a motorcycle going down the street are "jamming." Except that every night she brought him soaps.

"Where did you get those soaps?"

They were lavender, sandalwood, and ordinary scents you smell in ordinary brands; there were jasmine, sandalwood, and vanilla.

"Where did you get those soaps?"

Eventually things started bothering him. He found himself washing too much. He found her asking too much. She was wild but now she seemed like a stray cat, the way she was trying too hard and in cheap, fake ways to make his house theirs. So that with a brash, fragrant arm he waved her out of his life.

That is what happened in the inner city one time between a well-muscled man and a wild young woman, as I have heard it related to me by a friend, whose relative is the man. I thought it worth telling.

A History of the Wealthy World

Krishna conducted the Saint Louis Symphony, a primal debut, a "Borax of music," and it was well attended, somewhat well attended, with the thousands, the hearty thousands, leading each his train of stunning admirers to this rampage of a concert, this primal gala, the orchestra led by Krishna.

But this is the low point of our narrative now, because right in the middle of Fidelio the bats were released by evil-thinking snobs and barraged the conductor's eminence with their bumpless flappings. Our flighted cousins released upon the orchestra all manner of normal products, producing vertigo and loss of beat.

Woe to the situation! There was no saving it now, not with that Krishna paling beyond godhood to a wisp of history, not with the wealthy thousands stammering for change.

But Christ of the Waters appeared and flattered the assembly, reduced groping to zero, helped legions overcome their bumbling.

But Mohammed! stood aghast! at the princely falseness of it all and smashed his forehead on the balustrade. "For the glory and the moment, for the glory and the glory," he said, "see this as depth of folly unparalleled. See this as the decrepit poking-at-bums of a civilization on its deathbed. See this as sorry indeed, as bats over Krishna. As bats over Krishna!" he said, smashing his head.

"I reject," said Moses, "these hunkfuls of punk verbiage. I reject," he said, a little unsteady, "this broom."

The real savior was of course John Fitzgerald Kennedy, shot-dead President of the United States, because he introduced all manner of

legislative improvements to the wreckage of a simple civilization—
"Come," he seemed to say, "become now America the introspective,
caress yourselves with indecision, get fucked double-time by the
standard messiahs of your parentage, for the alternative is a stunning bulimia.

BAD DAY ON THE MOON

Unk, who is heavy, is not so heavy on the moon, which is the famous moon, extolled by the many in so many parables, sharp parables, and in the soft, ill-placed coos of struggling lovers. Unk, who is not heavy on the moon, looks a little like an overbaked bread loaf, what with his ways....

This moon is 3284 kilometers thick with 1000 kilometers between any point the next point of merit. Its inhabitants are exactly three: Unk, myself, and Lady George, a watcher from the bad bumps. "Confound it!" Lady George is saying. "I never thought I'd misplace *that*." Fortunately for us, Lady George is unprofessional. But woe to us if she catches on!

A terrible thing, this tension of bonds, because for goodness in its nightgown, only Lady George has any real pus among us. Look at us. We're three born-for-the-blossom naifs, except for Lady George, who has some real pus among us. Grant her that. Do not reduce her throes to spontaneity or bedevil her witchery with "combat," a term of reproach. So she's a watcher. So she makes sure we sink ourselves to the knees in duty, waddling out only in case of snake or vine, of which there are none on the moon. So what. She has some real pus.

Now grant this trainee a perfect hang. That's it, I am hanging. Good. Well thank you: while I was hanging I perceived the bubble nature, a little part of it green and desirable, right outside my hanging-spot, and I thought some very nice things (about it), because I'm essentially a very good person, and I also waited a few moments in the trough of peace for the slurping of cosmic reindeer (who didn't come, but nevertheless, it was a nice moment)—so thank you for the chance. You are immensely sweet.

"Luscious even," Unk insists. "I insist you use the word 'luscious.'"

"Oh, Unk," I say. "These are regular people reading this. They're not your typical sittin'-on-the-moon wise guys! They're not gonna get it if we start slipping in our tonguing-around-in-crotch symbolism here. Unk. Have a normal heart."

"Pus!" he says to me finally, sideways, his eyes glaring like mortal zippers. "Go shoot the zipper. God blemish the blemish. See what Unk will do. See just what."

"What will Unk now do?" I say patiently, hand on hip.

"I will *stomp your gravestones*!" He stamps his feet furiously.

"Oh." I stare at Unk with horror in my eye, though only in my eye, because I'm quite used to his excuses for digression from duty, and Lady George isn't around. It is best to amuse him with predictable reactions, though it is in actuality unnecessary to do anything at all. That's how it is. He is insane but has a lot of beautiful energy. He is a valued member of our team, of which I am the trainee.

Lady George is at the window. That is bad. *"So Lady George!"* I am wheezing, coughing and belching blood in great slow waves, a trick I learned from my uncle. *"Shall we have a relationship?"*

That clears her eyes. "Indeed we shall, you sweet, you bustle-ridden crotch-tonguer. We shall dance a swell mid-August on the mineral-bedevilled moon! We shall have our water with the proper dejection. We shall mourn that…'darned apocalypse.'" I am relieved to hear her litany.

"There you go." I am all smiles, creases, bumps. I move her right along—"Right along, Lady George"—and another dismal day on the moon begins.

Mercurio arrives. "Excuse me, sir—but are you the underdog?"

REVOLUTION'S MOMENTS

Burdensome unrest. That was the problem with the awkward situation as it presented itself to the scrutiny of presidents, ministers,
charges d'affaires. "A ho! unwieldy plan there, little situation. I'd say
revolution was right out, right out." But our tender and awkward
situation did not deem itself a heady fountain of fantastic changes,
nor on the other hand a blue amnesia. It had been purchased, this
situation of internal turmoil, its body had been plundered, this
exciting configuration, often often. So that now, alone in the fre-
quentation of miseries that its concealed cohorts insisted upon....
"Come avoid," the ministers were saying to those who would listen,
who were legion. "The path to avoidance is a breeze." What could the
situation offer in balance? What was there to compete with avoidance, that a little situation full of misery could suggest? So the
energetic little situation subsided, went limp, the tautness disappeared from its crying arms, and Mamby

Grief
Glockenspiel
Burnoose-Heat
Crimestopper

Floringula

Pestilence

and Joseph

went sailing into the dark dread of their horrible ends: loosely,
without overcoats, angrily—into the unsituated moments of everaf-
ter. (The Ministry—a full Christmas wreck, Beware!)

My country, Peru. Sign-bearer of the throbbing-sad world of excru-ciating poverty, rumpled with all the diversions from destiny and pockmarks of precipitating evils that are the hallmark of the throb-bing-sad world, a world run over by all sorts of plagues—Peru is my country.

My country, Peru. Great in its moments, and no one can see any lack of viable futures. Openness of possibility, the hallmark of ad-vance of a country.

One thousand slaughtered last year.

It is not a possible word, that we do not feel it. Yet that is the word of the world! Yet that is not possible! that we do not feel it. Yet that is what they say!

"Comeuppance deserved!"

But I and my country will answer. We feel it, we who are rumpled, and we will stoutly answer. For our bloody deeds.

Listen: When you are alone on a walk, and you are at your best, and like a Peruvian your best is when you need only soften lightly an already staid demeanor, and so you are softening, softening, softening....When you are thus, and a woman accosts you, speaks naked of matters of good application, the well-applied eyebrow—notice the woman.

That is Peruvian wisdom.

When you and your cat are standing together, she black, you red-dish (or black, or cream)—notice the cat.

This we offer the people. For there are important, important things to see and great, great moments to have.

That is my country, Peru, and those are the things we say. We are stamped and pushed, and yet we speak. To you, the calmest of judges. To you, a series of gifts:

For the watcher of crystals: One day on your walk may be a lost day!
For the gangster: The life you must have is your own!
For you: Be kind!

In the beginning there were two parts, the natural and the supernatural. These became the parts of Robert's life. Robert appeared in nature but preferred the environment of ideas; intangibly stretched between poles even he did not recognize, his spirit connived and twirled until much of the moot was real.

Such occurred when Robert spoke. "Carmelita, my love, I know that it isn't often that this love is spoken; I know that seldom am I effusive toward you; but you mustn't be angry. Now that little hound of yours, with which, as you must know, I am quite fed up, will have to be jettisoned, repulsed utterly from our company, if there is to be any continuance—or even, I might say, any peace, any joy, any warmth. Do not, I beg, take me too harshly, but listen well."

"Robert," said Carmelita, whose eyes felt too tight in her head, "Robert, my love, do not become embroiled in your passions. We are two, you and I, we form a nation, it is good for us to be expressive of what we want, but not too expressive, for that is feral chaos. Please, my love, please."

"Carmelita," rejoined Robert so fast it made her breath catch, "you are too simple, my love, too simplistic, you simplify too much. Take now the example of Britain. Britain regards America thus: as a chihuahua regards a sheepdog. Frightening, looming large. A sheepdog with a deranged hypothalamus. Britain also, however, regards America thus: as a sheepdog regards a chihuahua. A chihuahua with a weakness for turpentine. Or take, as an alternate example, Carmelita, my love, the recent profusion of kidney stress among the middle classes...." And so on. The successful intellect of Robert whelms over Carmelita's pure rose of love; they are married and live off the coast of the Sea of Cortez.

As Robert's son Cortez grew to manhood, passing through the various stages of wetting and homosexuality, Robert espied more and more often a haze on the horizon. "Can you blame him?" he would think to himself, gazing at the horizon. "Of course he needs someone." And there would be haze. Or: "Well, the bladder when so tender is not tamed so well as later." Strong haze. Strong strong strong.

As Robert died, Cortez began to sire a son who turned out, for a change, to be a brilliant thinker, an inventor of algorithms and a destroyer of frameworks. He promised worlds from the very start, wetting his crib in floral helices, sucking the breast in wild but precise rhythmical abandon. Later he travelled much and the fatal cold he caught in London did not claim him before he had had the chance to sire twins, Sarah and Gore.

Sarah is the focus of this piece, an aphrodisiac piece. Sarah had beautiful breasts, ribs, buttocks, thighs, calves, knees, elbows, toes, ears, eyes, ankles, heels, palms, and wrists; she was an aphrodisiac. She flowed like a tsunami, always on the graceful go. She was a behavioral psychologist and existential philosopher, though in a way she was angry at everything. Sometimes, to spite her upbringing, she would promenade nude on the Sea of Cortez's coast.

Afterwards many other men and women were born, some of Sarah and her children and their children and others of Gore and his children and those children's children too. The television was turned off to ensure a good home environment.

"You know," Castroviejo said to Casanueva, his sister, "if you want to do something, you must imagine to yourself that people will like whatever it is. Otherwise you are a criminal against your image of humanity, regardless of humanity's feelings. Yes?" he said, to ensure attention.

"Yes yes yes. Castroviejo, yes yes."

"In that case," said Castroviejo, "Fichte becomes meaningless. Fetch me my pipe." And so on.

All of this was quite natural, quite natural indeed.

Unusual Sight

I was coursing down my boulevard, a tidy affair with rows of smooth-brick huts on either side stretching into the boundaries of vision down by the cesspools and communal other, and I couldn't help noticing they'd erected a tunnel in the middle of the air. It was kept up there with a set of struts and buttresses that resembled nothing so much as the patterns of sun in *Train*, by Monet, and as I thought of that work a heavy rumbling between the street in front of me and the street after that began and I wondered was there action, and where, in the tunnel? When I got to the spot of rumbling it had shifted, down I think to where I'd been before, but when I doubled back and stood agape the rumbling had shifted once more. Phooey, I said, and tried to hear the rumbling again. But just then I heard my boss trumpeting dominance over his megaphone and I set out at once for the place of my employment.

In the rec room I asked a lady about the system of tunnels, and she said she'd heard of no such thing, and I said okay, there's only one tunnel, it's going down my boulevard through the air, right smack dab in the middle of what is a very well-balanced affair with rows of smooth-brick huts guiding one's eye to the city's filth, and she said oh, you must mean the C-bahn, over there near the community discharge place, and yes, I must, I said, but what's the C-bahn, and she said there is, in the course of the progress of humankind one time in time when death speaks straight to all and that is what the C-bahn is, though for now it seems to be sticking to your street alone.

Right at the corner around which I would see the C-bahn I stopped to buy some Toothsome Piglets and rehearse the meaning of C-bahn. But when I came forth, the C-bahn was gone, so I walked on home, glancing at space, wondering why, why death had chosen to speak to me and my friends on the boulevard, for though we had eyes and thoughts and souls we were by no means all of the world, not at all the whole entire thing, and I figured death must be waiting, testing the waters, so I decided to give him no quarter, and whenever anyone in the street would bring up the tunnel on struts I would shrug my shoulders and look across the street.

GRACE

Anders has redecorated the kitchen! This stabs me in the back a mighty pain, for that boy once told me only on my recommendation would he alter this, the kitchen. But a boy is a boy and Anders has purchased icetrays for a whopping, whopping seven hundred and fifty dollars apiece. They are special icetrays. Each one holds ice but in a pattern: perhaps a goofy face, as these do. In each is a goofy face.

Enter misarmed Chip. Chip walks in and we show him the trays, we say do you like and he says, he says it doesn't look like him—he's annoyed at our japes. Anders and I look at each other and shrug. Poor misarmed Chip.

"I have a Q.I.D.," says Chip. "That is my degree." We smile to indicate our readiness for punch, but Chip stands looking out the window. Anders and I shrug. Every once in a while, often after a particularly harsh confession (he is a rigorous Catholic), Chip gets it into his head that he is being suborned by systems unworthy of his sacrifice. At such junctures he plots out a system of merits to adorn him properly; this time we have the Q.I.D., it seems, at the peak, and there must be various other symbols below. That is for Chip.

"When I was a child," says Chip, "my father was ruthlessly beaten. My mother remarried and my new father heeded her advice. He bought a Mazerati. He located his carpets in Denver. But I was never alike. I was never, never alike."

Anders gets a rag and I continue to inspect the kitchen. With the rag Anders wipes off Chip's face. In the kitchen I find a spatula and with it I heap Chip's face into a heap in the middle. Anders reclines against me and I laze an arm over his shoulder. He tilts back his head and says, "We should really do something for Chip besides this. He's a very sad creature."

"We have to do it," I say. "Perhaps someday we'll be able to exhibit kindness. At the moment this is the only way. Sleep well and enjoy your blessings."

"Enjoy your blessings," Anders says. "Yes."

DETACHMENT

An eclogue for the New Age

I am living alone among the weeds, because nettles (boiled, as prescribed for hard living by an early Nazi doctor) contain all vital nutrients.

My shack is substandard but I subsist beautifully on the effluvia of my friend Nature. She foams and farts and I live. We have a *silent understanding*.

I also have a profession, which changes things but slightly.

My profession is still considered by some to be substandard. Despite its proven effectiveness in eliciting tender behavior from even the most drunk, my profession is often considered not blameless. Despite the legions who relax to our touch, my fellows and I are often hounded.

I am a masseur. We live in an angry, ineffective age, one in which might slaughters innocence, and I massage the impotent to relaxation, strength and power. I do this by the only means I have available: the kneading power of my hands.

I also speak. Speaking is essential. "By means of speech a good masseur can elicit bodily pops from his subject," said my master. This is absolutely true.

"Imagine the gardens of your delight, even the gardens of his imperial highness, the highest gardens of the world, in which the imperial highness takes his stroll, stroll stroll in the wooded acreage, gazing at the sights, the well-creeped trellis on the hard-won arch, oh that imperial highness, gazing at the metropolis of bedbugs polishing the imperial silver (mock castles, mock temples, a lakebed for the glinting silver, high-glinting in this strolling afternoon, one can pretend the bedbugs are doing 'the gondola')...."

I am fixing the muscles of a fine young lass, they too tense, she lost among crazy angers. I try to get her to "come around," to realize her puniness, the impossible smallness of her enthusiasms.

"Now this is the finest garden of all, the garden of detachment, where detachment is all, just keep that shoulder loose, you always get a knot there, you bitch....The garden of detachment, the ultimate garden, the ultimate relaxation, where the emperor, his imperial highness, beheads his loyal subjects....Detachment is necessary for these, his loyal subjects, because of the flow and jittery progressions of the numina....Because of that, because of the high art beyond the cosmic spherodrome....Because of that, here it is detachment, no other answer. Do you see? The imperial highness is breathing the perfect air. Relaxed."

The fine young lass shudders to icy stillness, the alignment perfecting itself, finally, here in her shoulders, where I cause her to shudder. I am gazing out the window at the good balance of the elements of the natural environment. Somewhere I feel my smile, a reassuringly unchanging, ever-perfect concatenation of felicitously straight lines, the teeth just showing their perfect edges, the sides of the smile pushing up the cheeks into knots, tiny round centerings of all my tension, which I must fling away too, at some point....I am happy with my smile because it seems cruel, though it is not. It is just a delirium of angered tepidity, which I encourage the treatable world to be, and the honesty of its apparent message—"I am angered, I am tepid; I would boil, but I'm tepid," as my master's surface mantra went—is, so far as I am concerned, perfect.

The fine young lass accompanies me to my still hut among the weeds. She is dismayed by my substandard life but clings to my neck. "Perhaps you really will solve all the problems of the coming age," she suggests.

"Perhaps I will," I say. "Perhaps I will."

THE APPROPRIATE ENDEAVOR

The juice was special; the air breathed through lace, for this was a lace occasion; and Todd was heavy in his suit. "Howdy."

The dowager smoothed her breast.

But no one could see! The three androgynous halfwits were spinning in vicious circles as the President spoke of might. "This day we have might; we have radars in our base, and blood within our tanks. We have superlative masters of the arts of wreaking. We have glossaries of indignation and hell"—his voice grew weepy as if with sentiment—"we have madness.

"But gentlemen, yes gentlemen, and ladies—we have, we have dissembling too. Those three"—he pointed at the halfwits—"though who could tell, those three dissemble no end. They"—he pointed again—"give no breath to virtues, no quantities to success. They ignore, they ignore even me.

"And if you ask them"—he stood akimbo—"they'll give you backwards, flipped-up, malignacious answers." The whole room gasped and then there was big silence. Todd was heavy in his suit and the lace breathed through the air; the juice was very special. "Howdy," Todd whispered again to the dowager, who was in diamonds. "Howdy and I am Todd. Todd Perspective."

The dowager sniffed the air. "A good point hot in here, not not?"

Todd, despite his meager education, realized the lady was speaking wrong. He smoothed his hair and began again. "Howdy and I am Todd. Todd Perspective." Same answer verbatim. He smacked her hard with a palm and continued as if nothing were amiss, and as if the President were listening: "I am Todd Perspective and I am in from Washington, the capital. I sneeze at phony perspectives. I scoff at fact-mongerers and lynchpin-yodelers. Does this describe you— are you the object here?"

The dowager was yodeling for help. The President was speaking: "And besides these, these 'three'"—he pointed at the halfwits—"we have a 'lady.' Now she, this 'lady,' says she's married to the famous head of this or that. She gives her money to our enterprise, as does this reputed husband. But look at her." The room with one head swivelled on his finger to the dowager. "She's ugly." The room erupted in screams of delight. "She bears no end of sick craze in that moony head of hers, you can just tell, eh eh eh?" The crowd nodded. "And. She's sick."

The dowager by this time was sobbing wildly and clutching Todd's breast (she had decided danger occurred only when she spoke). Todd was ill at ease in this position but could by no means uproot a sobbing lady in her majority. But then a wind possessed her and she spoke: "President, hey President, the air withal smacks of deliberation in flagrante. The muck, the migrations: your badness."

Todd swivelled, smacked, and rested. The President clapped. Todd danced about in little circles and the President's hands slowed as in a nightmare. "This ah Perspective, on the other hand"—the whole air tensed with the weight of what was to be said—"is pretty good. He smacks the appropriate malignacious. He undoes with palms the swiping of goodwill. He notices the affidavits." Applause, but short. "He's awful!" Wild, wild cheering.

The dowager sobbed, and Todd was laid to rest at the end of days with due ceremony in a lace-and-creme wake in the capital. Soon the President began inviting ministers and judges to assess and praise his competence and that of his countrymen.

ESCAPE FROM PARIS

As told by Daniil Ilyushin whilst on the high seas

It was a slow, swaying motion that held our Paris that night, our Paris dotted with slow-swaying lights, an occasional lever, *grincement de lèvres*....I grabbed onto the post and slid down it, giddy with the personal nature of the acceleration involved: I slid to the street.

Burst tubes, ramshackle moments lined up like huts for rats, the softness of the steely ground's decay—these things I saw. Mme. Ronsard was looking for me. "In which section does Ronsard live?" I was wholly alone! An elevator left me with too much nausea; a janitor emerged. "I'm the adventurer," he said. "But where is Mme. Ronsard?" I asked. There was ample contempo living here, he indicated with his smile. But who among us knows? I offered with my hand. The sculptor knows, he hurled with his eyes. Perhaps I should kill you, I mentioned with my knife. "She lives in a flat alone. A reasonable, well-kept arrangement which contributes, I am told, to the nature of grace in her soul. She will see you if you can find her." And with that, the malingering janitor vanished.

Who has not told of the frights and abuses, the long-term wrenchings that start in a lonely search? Perhaps the ground is of interest. The ground was of steel, soft shiny steel, decaying with the passage of the moon each night, the sunlit face of that august globe the doom of metal surfaces....Perhaps you would jump at my memory, my dainty memory of the churlish Pierre, churlish Pierre in his disarray, a longing for moments fast on his fish-bum face.

Perhaps you would love that I told him, I mentioned the moments with my arching brows, I trounced his awe with a dollop of truth— along your streets! along your streets, a profusion of moments! more moments than Byzantine clerics in Turkey! more matter for thought than hair.

Mme. Ronsard is bathing. She gazes at the workmanship of her cameos, delighting in the fever of their contours, the slurs implied in their gilt, and thinks how lucky she is. It is I who barge in. "Daniil, you must fetch me the key." I gaze at her profoundest face and produce an envelope. She opens it, reads the note, and returns to her exquisites. "Yes," she says, "the curls unite with the crosiers. Yes, that is certainly true. I see it now."

Oh my! I've inflated! I have billowed, to be precise. I am an empty sheet, fine and black, veiling this woman's reality. I am wet to the crotch but my eyes are on fire—and the strange Mme. Ronsard is fainting! Every moment closer, she knows it will happen, like a sneeze. It does and I course through the roof, an apparition through roofs, and find my way through the many glistening streets of midmorning Paris. My friends are waiting on quays, eager and happy, on quays all over, I am rich, I have friends, they stomp the quays, they are glorious, the quays are all full, I have friends, I am out, completely, of Paris.

TIA CARRO AND HER BABIES

The work I'm involved in demands a hell of a lot of respite, and no one's giving me respite. I mean, let me glance at the ways of the supers, let me think about respite the way they think about respite, and soon I'll be a loony loony. Betcha.

Ever know an armful of babies? Sixteen. Sixteen babies, puling and teething and screaming baby oaths at me, lucky I'm a witch. An armful of babies, on the beach (we're going to the beach say today), is one unpleasant burden. Puling and teething and screaming baby oaths at me, lucky I'm a witch. And the water, so cold! As if begging one to shiver away one's coquetry.

I got a husband, his name is Mud, he always wants to know things. He asks the time in Washington, I take a guess, he slaps me and says "I gotta *know*, baby. I gotta know because that's my moniker, based on knowledge, people think I know, got it? My moniker. My moniker."

He doesn't come to the beach, though. He has important business with his friends, who aren't really friends but special merchants, merchants of the near-impossible. I go to the beach and think about the babies while the sky falls down and my whiplash— sometimes my whiplash acts up. I tell you.

My name is Tia Carro and my bus number is 803, that's for the bus, which I take to travel around on with my babies, it's the only form of public transportation cheap enough and tolerant enough for me and my babies. Right now my babies are puling and it's something terrible, really awful.

My husband Mud doesn't take the bus, he always hitches rides with his special cronies and adepts, he trains people that's why he's got adepts, so we're never together even though I cook him dinner. Even though something really interesting happened involving all my babies I hardly ever have anything to think about.

Easy Time

The commissioner stood by the pulpit, part of his length to its right, a respectful distance, and spoke of the death. "The church has been injured!" he said. "These walls, so essential to our lives, are stained with blood. Our grief is not only for the slain, but for our church, and therefore for ourselves." He spoke for fifteen minutes.

The church was built mainly of stone and the nave, in which the commissioner spoke, was faced with marble. The altar behind the pulpit was flanked by two freestanding columns and two half-embedded in the far wall. On the front of the structure was a miniature frieze with a heart surrounded by gilt rays. The columns were made of marble and were grooved and adorned in the doric manner. It was at these that a man in the congregation looked as the commissioner spoke of the death.

"I will not allow anyone to say that our state is not helping the causes," the commissioner finished.

"Long live the state," the congregation said.

"I'm sad," the man said to his wife, in the evening.

"Why is that?" she said.

"I saw those columns today," he said. "They make me sad."

"It's the death," his wife said. "A time for sadness."

The man drank some soup. "I almost grew up in that church."

His wife stirred a pot.

"To me it's alive," the man said. "You know that. Sometimes I talk to it. But those columns..."

"Be careful," the woman said to herself, having splashed some soup on her hands.

"It isn't a church," the man said.

"Shut up," his wife said. "We'll talk in bed."

"No," the man said. "In bed I fuck."

"How hard?" his wife asked.

"Very hard."

"All right," his wife said. "Very hard. Soup's hot."

"You're funny," the man said. "But that's what this is. Funny."

"Shut up," his wife sang. "Shut up, shut up, shut up. You big dildo, shut up."

After the meal they wrestled about and the man overpowered his wife and afterward they lazed about in bed until daybreak.

Adjective Death in the West

In the lacy dawn three burly young men in white suits were shuffling down the dew-fixed main road to the railway station. Their brief-cases, brown. Pens, handmade tortoiseshell. Not a one spoke, and on each a look of thoughtful houndedness as he passed the brilliant signs touting nails, good times and drink. "FANTASTIC PENETRATING METAL MAKES YOUR INTERLOCKING PARTS INTO ONE." "SCREAM-RIPPING DAYS AND SERENE INNER JOY AT THIS WELL-BUTTRESSED HOUSE OF ENTHUSIASM." "STOUT DRUNKS WITH OUR ABLE DRINKS."

No bumping and shoving as the men passed the signs; no silent derision as seeking critiques became fishing for compliments. Instead there prevailed among them a feeling of greatness curtailed, common destiny languidly upended at its peak by spiritual vaga-bonds.

Their efforts, though doomed, had seen the light of at least a few eyes, for at least a few days.

"I dunno," one said, eyeing a root beer ad. "Quality like Jake's doesn't just happen every day."

"Nope," another one said, "there's no accounting for lexical whizzes."

"That's right," the first one said. "The world is the sorrier."

Jake smiled wistfully. "Too kind, too kind. But we all have the gift," he said softly.

At this the three men turned up the left corners of their mouths and plodded on in silence for a while.

"Do you think it will ever be the same?" Jake asked into the road getting steadily shorter.

"Nope," one said.

"Nope," the other said.

"We were given the drug to harass realities," the first one said, "to fix them with chrome, the harsh chrome of our languid turtle. Putting one thing in front of the other."

His comrades looked at him sideways for a moment with wide-open eyes, then smiled at the road, and then the smiles faded back into the melancholy that planed just over the dust.

"Well, they won't see our likes again," the first man said.

"They've fixed their shit a hundred years back," the third one said.

"Look out," Jake said.

It was old Billy Drake, on a roof up ahead, doing what he must, and the writers knew well what that was.

"Who do you think that is?" the first man said.

"I'd say it was something on a roof," the third one said.

"I'd say you were right," Jake said, and the three walked on.

"A man called Drake," Jake said a few moments later, "I think I might say."

"I'd say that was right," the first man said.

"He's up on the roof," the third man said.

"He's up on the roof," the first man said.

"Look out," Jake said.

"You are gettin' outta town!" Drake yelled. *"Hounded out! The goners! The previous men!"*

"Heyyy!" someone else yelled. *"Heyyy!"*

The writers turned and looked sluggishly at the start of a mob. They did not flinch. The station was yards away.

"   Bibles for   ed Folk," the sign on Drake's roof now read.

"Sleeping outdoors!" Drake yelled.

The writers were tired.

"Go out! Go out! Go out!" the town yelled.

And then it dissolved in guffaws and yelps and giggles.

And the three men, sitting on a bench, had their solitary thoughts, and thought of the sad, sad age, and how time would stand still, and how writers would now be made, not born, and all of knowledge abandoned. It was the end of Voice.

"There's no accounting for taste," Jake said as the train pulled in.

"There's no accounting for taste," the other two said.

A Wisdom Tale

The master comes prancing steadily toward the light, cheering with his lips. He's subtle in the glow and all the disciples commend him. "A perfect man, the proctor." "A decidedly beautiful doctor." "O for a bishop as plain as our priest." "This ninja could render to blood any beast." As night falls the liquids are turned; the seven young men assume position. "Prance, prance, prance."

"I'm going to Nurnberg on the first cart out."

"And Susie?"

"She'll have to keep."

"What about the cats?"

"They'll have to keep."

"And Clarence?"

"He's manning the Arkansas convoys. Muscular."

The master is going to travel. The seven young men bring gifts of well-wishing—potatoes endives cups a reticule stew-hands—and thirteen honest beads. "As you hit the road you take what we need. Assure yourself of a great return."

The master is thinking. A great return./ A sensuous urn./ A banal kern/ in the fields by Nurn-/ berg, scribed with the information we'd kill for.

The master celebrates his wife's pleasure. He's promised her a gilt spoon carved with his initials and she has planted kisses on his happy fingers.

The cart pulls out with a mighty creak of rods and levers. The master closes in on a burlesque novel and for hours there is nothing.

The fog falls over the land and keeps breath hovering for the cartmates, many of whom are weirdos; the master himself is lost.

In Nurnberg the master buys some things he needs and looks at the relics, shrouding himself in anonymity as he communes with history. Finally he hops on a cart back to those who need him. As his destination looms he gets to thinking. A great return....I'll sit up in elegance. I'll hold my carriage just slightly off-kilter, that ought to throw the certainty enough to let a new glimmer through, a glimmer of excellence or something, something new....I'll hold up the spoon by my nose. For years they'll remember; I'll make it plain.

He arrives at the load-point and it is chargingly, resoundingly empty. There is no one and the armature of the weirdos leaving the cart is solidly entrenched. Ye weirdos, the master thinks. Ye weirdos leaving so well-entrenched in armature....Where are his people?

A cat jumps out of the adjoining field and pounces on the master. He caresses the smoothness of its flanks and mumbles his woe. "I've never had this happen," he says to the cat. "Others have always been there to feed and caress me. I am the master."

"I need a master," the cat says. "Mine is picking strawberries."

The master's legs feel sudden nostalgia. "Well I'm a ninja," he tells the cat. "And a bishop. I need a bishopric."

"I have the likes of that. I'm no parvenu."

The master is smiling, almost prancing now. He pats the cat and smiles, pats and smiles. "A great return,/ a sensuous urn..." The cat looks into his eyes and the master sees discipleship and trust. The master is back in practice.

Six young men jump onto the platform from out of the adjoining hamlet. They are sorry; their fellow young man misinformed them about the train in order to forestall the master's return and muck things up a bit, to prove some point or other. They and the women who follow admire the master and the cat he is patting. The disciples ask things and the master answers. He mentions many things and as they start off for home he looks back fondly at the cat prancing steadily toward its strawberry-picking master, God knows where, but somewhere...thank God.

COARSE HOME EVENT

Mike began a description of the afterlife. "There will be a panoply of angels. These will be graded rank-and quality-wise. The topmost one will speak to the bottommost ones with a grating voice, saying 'Here we must live forever.' The newcomer dead will recoil in horror from such a tepid first view of the glory of God. The newcomer will have thought of Tintoretto and Blake, and the love of insubstantial things in Jung, will have concentrated his being on the worlds to come in all their teeming perfections, and will instead see wilt.

"But then, the excitement of the chase!"

Pavel removed his clothes and lay on the bed for Joseph to judge. Joseph thought the chest a little too expansive. Moreover the thighs were disproportionate to the calves and waist. But the waist taken alone was a gem. Perhaps, Joseph thought, if I lay down next to him, I could overcome my judgmental feelings toward him. Perhaps I would feel less inclined to criticize what he can control so poorly. Perhaps then I would understand his plight and wish to configure to it better. But perhaps not, and he has hardly invited me. I could not lie down!

Pavel noticed Mike behind Joseph. Pavel was about to speak to Joseph on the subject of the possibility of inspectional mutuality when Mike began speaking hoarsely about the Revolution. "It was an angry affair, huge swarming brakes of soldiers lunging at every breach in the oppressives' fortifications. Certain men did not understand the significance of the anger and wished to curtail it, did not understand the force of the hatred and wished to undo it, did not see the fine ways. Other men were gung-ho and ludicrous, acting out the female in their personal manners together, eye-contact highs and boot-bumps to scatter the fear, even contact of blunter form such as arms on the torso, necks nearly entwined.

"And then, the Revolution a success, we endeared the race to our ways and encouraged happiness, which succeeded and caused us our greatest victory, longevity of regime."

Mike did not go away and Joseph felt angry. He got up and strode toward Mike. Still Mike did not move. He was looking at Pavel and at Pavel's nudity. Joseph arrived at Mike and confronted him broadside. "Mike," his body seemed to be saying, "you are more than we need. Too much, right now. There is, in you, which you represent, a superfluity of presence. Various things. Your notions and knowledge and fast-racing-toward-the-ultimate mind, your clever ways and directness: all too much! There is simple here, there is a certain simple, a glorious nothing, a fragment of naught, a constipation void, just a tiny mundane zero, and you are too much." Pavel lay nude on the bed. His thighs were actually quite entrancing, and his chest was "magnificent." His abdomen could have laid waste the monarchy. Only his neck was a little too short, much too little of it really, it was almost too much the way his head and shoulders blended together, it gave him an air of being uneducated, which he happened to be, though there is no reason to suppose that he must have been. It was a false signal, nothing of any basis, and those who would have supposed his lack of education from his neck are quick to judge, so it is a pity his neck was that way.

Later, Joseph lay on the bed next to Pavel and Pavel described Joseph's buttocks. "Three of them," Pavel said. Joseph shifted. "Perhaps you misunderstood me," Pavel repeated; "I said 'Three of them.'" Joseph turned over and rubbed his eyes. "Three of them?" Joseph asked. "Yes," Pavel said, "three of them."

THE GLORIOUS CONTRIBUTION OF ACADEMIA TO THE TWENTY-FOURTH CENTURY

It is a quiet room in a well-charmed land. The thirty men in black and brown are assembled with steady faces, awaiting the good entrance of Professor Bung.

The clock opens another hour and Bung walks in. Applause resounds from his shininess, which he quickly stows beneath an impenetrable aura of hominess. As a homeslice, Professor Bung is calm and genteel. As a lecturer, he is seething fire.

A man in black introduces him. "It is..." The audience cheer.

Then it is Bung. "Gentlemen! It is with enormous pleasure that I open a chapter, a chapter of goodwill and truth, in the rollicking annals of the Fantasma Glee Club.

"Today we are of course investigating an entirely well-known phenomenon: the existence of the horde. The horde, as we define it, is the grouping of like-minded individuals in pursuit of some sort of spiritual satisfaction. We are, for example, a horde.

"The character of this present horde, however, is significantly unlike that of others, the hordes of the past, even of the hoary past. We have involved in our workings a new idea, a new concept: the well-blown individual. Each of us here is a clear-thinking, high-meaning, darkness-avoiding, sempiternally-vowed individual of the highest rank: that is, well-blown. The well-blown individual does not suborn his enthusiasms to the discretions of others: he is so well possessed of their control that there is no need. Discipline is therefore a silly appendix. And of course a horde of well-blown men is hardly a horde at all: at least not in the sense that word was given in the dowdy, conscious past. This horde is special. That is why we call it a horde.

"Now we all know"—gentle glances at the confreres—"that among those in other hordes, there is seldom any subtlety. That in those hordes, in which men are forsworn to paths, there is seldom any subtlety. That the speech of the mouth is often lost in the twistings of the innards which result from their lack of proper maintenance in the face of decomposition, which decomposition is of course ascribable to hypocrisy, blasphemy, and decrepitude—of the speech of the mouth. The whole degeneration has as ultimate origin a decision to value comfort over fun. Fun, fun, fun—do you remember?"

At this formula the other members of the Glee Club shout out in unison: "Fun, fun, fun—we are devoted!"

"And that," Bung concludes, "is just what we must be given over to: the nurturance of fun."

"Objection!" comes a darkling voice from the rear. All faces turn in ugly shock. It is a little man clad in brown. "I give you the Goths!"

For a while there is nothing. Then Professor Bung dares a response. "And I, dear sir, give you…the French!"

At this a cackle arises across the crowd. Bung hides a right-sided smile in his water, breathes distress, and begins his conclusion. "I would like to point out an odd historical fact which, I hope, will provide some enthusiasm—some meaning—for our neverending battle on behalf of fun. In the days of drums and armies, when men carried swords, guns, and helmets, there was a technique for inducing the men to continue. It was called rhythm. The rhythm was played out on a drum, and it had a certain order very clearly defined to generate ripples of forward eagerness. It was rrrat, rrrat, rrrat tat tat—rrrat, rrrat, rrrat tat tat…" Someone cheers. "Here it is on the table." The Professor taps out the rhythm on his lectern, five times. At the end can be heard two or three soft voices from the audience: "Yes."

"This was the rhythm of marching. I think by now you understand: the three rolls are for moving; the 'tat tat' at the end of the third is an anticlimax in sore need of resolution; and the silence denies the resolution, only to furnish, with the arrival of the next set of rolls, rrrat rrrat, a momentary respite from the prison of anticipation. This musical juggernaut rolls on, on, on, and the soldiers are the braver because of it.

"This, friends, is a smidgen we can garner from our trove of facts about the previous hordes. They were cruel, but their achievements were great and from them we may profit.

"Speed safely and have a good night. Fun, fun, fun—we are devoted!"

"Fun, fun, fun—we shall become!" And each good man is off to his good wife, whom he instructs; and well they sleep, full to brimming with the new understanding, insight, and philosophy.

DEVIL IN THE BATHROOM

He returned home and went through every room in the house, searching, searching for the devil, for the devil, he knew, might be anywhere. Actually he only felt the devil might be anywhere; he knew that devils didn't exist, just as everyone knows that devils don't exist. But he began with the kitchen; then he looked at the bedroom; then he went to the living room, full with a couch and credenza; then he tried the windows to make sure they were shut, and they were; then he sat upon the couch hard by the credenza. A devil could easily do you in, he thought as he sighed relief. A devil could do you in and leave no trace. He had read about a devil that had killed the young King Edward, a former King of England, by a red-hot poker inserted into his rear. A similar devil could be equally traceless in its work, he felt as he sighed relief.

But there he was in the bathroom, that devil. Just sitting there, waiting. So out he came, that devil, and did him in. It wasn't a pretty sight; it was sordid, a spectacle for bloodthirsty eyes. But there was a groan, for the devil had done him only partially. As he struggled to regain consciousness, certain silver and sere spots crowded his eyes and so after a while he decided it was all over; he was prepared to "give up the ghost." He did not "give up the ghost," however: this was not "in the cards." He groaned once more and entered a coma.

Much, much later he had trouble with correction fluid and girls. The first he would brush away with arabesque twists of the hand, but there it would be: correction fluid, and lots. And then there were girls. Many called at his door, and they were too young. Soon he gained in virility and the girls went away in some fear.

"What do you want of me?" he asked his wife one day. "Do you believe that I am a machine, a mechanism for your enjoyment intended? Is it your thought that your whims are my standing orders, my sallying commands? that in me you have a true and loyal servant of your tiniest wants? A servant of your wants, is that what you think I am, a servant of your wants? Or do you see me rather as a knight, your chevalier, a paladin of yours, your Galahad? Is this it? Do you not realize that I am large, that I am not to be subordinate, that this is against the new thought? Can't you understand?" He held her gently by the neck. "Can't you? Baby-o? Hurbly-boony? Lurk-o-dram?" He dotted this with some quick contractions of his hands.

"Ack," his wife said, pulling free. Then she began: "There is no use arguing. We have lived a fairly short life together, we have a child, we are dotted by raves, we are pricks in the surface of smooth, smooth cosmos..."

"Get to the point," he said.

"I am wanting...I am wanting to urge dissolution. Divorce is the whim of the honest moment. I cannot urge other."

"Get out," he said.

The next seven years he spent wandering coasts, always an eye open for the old devil or whatnot. He had his fortune and enjoyed it completely, at which point he found a suitable man and received that man's money; he earned it.

The seven years after he started to age, upon which he longed for the girls. But there was the devil, and the man came up with some excellent plans.

THE TURK AND THE VIRUS

Okay, heaving the awful calabashes around was not dearth of horror, no terrorless strop, not a shine on novel Ferenczi's culotte—nor, when the legions succumbed to the rindpest, was joy to be had in the cold. There was not, in the following gargles, love and the peace of the monkey to toss and beleaguer, nor card-shining bunk to enroll in a flip. And when Jerzy ate rashes, who prinked and spun? What gut-dervish twists were the order, that day? What cut-rate cocottes?

That's it, there was sadness, talc sadness, core feebles, mat groans in the parsnip. That Joe, that Bob, that Jerzy, that novel Ferenczi, stitching their pants in the parsnip, lounging in green, gone gooey for cords—"My God, you stuck foul, how cut short, how despicable!"—thinking of all the ways to curtail yon virus, yon horrible life form, thinking of none—such sadness! talc sadness! core whoredom for all.

So we set up a Turk to get rid of the situation, we positioned him somewhere in between the two lines, put a dart on his shoulder and tied it down, referred to him secretly as "grunt" but called him officially "Hallelujah" after the refrain of the Hebrews, and there he was standing pretty secure-looking with his rocky gaze on the enemy and its trucks, and he really was the whole situation in a nut, he was even the world, at that point, when only the gasping of quarter malevolents could be heard at the crossing, when only the horrors of cold and crutch kept watch by the crossing, when only a pasty cabbie would laugh.

That Turk, the motions of gust and remorse, the holds of matted glee on his workingman's eye, all forms of the Turk, all forms of the

Turk—exciting! His liver, pools of awful deep blue, swarming with camels of Bogczi; his heart, the massing of flies on a quarterhorse; such lights on the ages, his parts!

The Turk, the Turk, spoke glowingly of his life at home, *Maedchen* and charming brother, the cunning of awful Sa'id, dispersal of silver at weddings, direction of Cornwall memories in elders ("No! the moose was not cooked!"), who'd been there, such terrible, terrible knowledge, there in that Turk, there in that Turk...

We languished, and there stood the Turk...

Months and months, long and wrecked...

The fear of derangement grappling with several of us: "Could he, say, in a fit of global warming, wrap his legs around one of us, say, and *change his mind?*" "Or even deliver the goods?" "Yank his old hard-widget pride through the muck?" And finally, Ivan: "Yes, we're dealing with a human being."

So we gave the Turk some bills and removed the dart from his shoulder and sniffed him out, found that he stank, gave him a shower, a pleasant affair with three soaps, and the Turk appeared to be washing as we wandered far into the scopes of the enemy, lounged on the crosshairs, and caught those awful flesh-scrappers right between our teeth. The Turk, we have heard, examined his life and became a false messiah, and there was certainly more about him but we have had a hard time recently and have rather enjoyed lying around in the cotton dust of his mills, which they say he has learned how to own, stropping his pureness on wealth, clicking that old cigar in his public teeth...

At the end, a mighty ovation. The beams ring out, the rivets shiver in their encasures, the sea trembles slightly, the sky gets lighter, the birds are ambushed right out of the sky, the whole place turns a little spooky but no matter, the applause is coming—and there's Oyster! Oyster on the high poop! Oyster with a face for relieving insomnia. Gloating like a pig's disease up high on the poop…The applause continues, it's a major ovation, and Oyster is smiling, and bowing, and yea the ovation swells, it's encore and bravo and lend me your plume, till the calls are riddled with claps and a new level rises, the texture is dense with claps over calls, and Oyster is bowing, he's smiling, Oyster is grinning completely, completely a grin, no end to grin, an endless swarm of teeth…

The audience calls! The audience claps! Encore! Bravo! Lend me your plume! Oyster perambulates, twirls an end, flicks a tiny symbol—the audience thrills and erupts in the headiest crush of love you've ever imagined…

Ex

Every day I have wondered aloud, "What is there going to be for me this day?" Every day I have gone to sleep, wondering "What has there been in this day for me?" Only now, twelve years later, do I realize the funkiness of my idiot. Robert has said to me, with anger, "You never make me anything. You sit around, holding your wang or some book, even worse, and cruise around with vagaries. I'm leaving on the next train to Baltimore."

Baltimore is where I lived, ten years. It was right in the middle of my Baltimore experience that I learned to ask myself those goofy questions every day. Then I moved out here. Robert is going to leave me now. He is going to go to Baltimore, where he will meet some fascist, lock him in an argument, and post him ante-bellum to the land of his unravelling. Just as he did with me.

I can't, of course, say that I was without idiot in the whole affair. Even semblances of justness are not my forte, nor even in my repertoire. Let me tell a story.

Robert came in one day, saying "Who is the mayor-elect?" I spoke then with modesty and determination, involving Robert and his private cronies in my answer. He dumped an egg on my head, some allusion, and spent the rest of the day sweeping and jacking off, I can't deny it, jacking off. All that night my arm wandered over to his back, only to be repulsed utterly by swivels of his neck. How hard is a man!

So you understand. It is not ideal, but it is better than his remaining.

Angry Suburb Story

Arch and Ron did not spring full grown from the womb. Neither did their sister, Czechoslovakia. Rather they cashed checks and washed the windows of Mercedes for a good many years before becoming who we know them for today, good attentive folk with a yen for the sixties.

"Here is the den," says Arch. He is fiddling with a knob attached to his elbow, or rather clinging to his elbow. He pulls it off and shrugs: "No one can tell you, these days."

Back in the kitchen, Marty, Macbeth and Pierce are choosing their foods. "This one will go well with cabbage; this one we'd better leave for last; this one has a great potential for disrupting the flow of our lives; this one is ruin to all concerned."

Ron, Arch's brother, is beckoning to a woman he knows as Deirdre. She has removed her blouse and is posing against the inner side of Ron's bedroom's door. Ron removes his shirt and examines her closely. She lets fall her skirt. Ron takes off his pants. They both remove their underwear. Now they are naked. Ron still beckons to Deirdre. Perhaps she will speak to him? Perhaps he will have it accomplished?

By eight o'clock the guests have gone. Arch and Czechoslovakia gasp and choke on the couches, exhausted. Ron is upstairs with Deirdre. Ron does not know the guests have gone. He would be embarrassed if he did and would rush down to Arch and Czechoslovakia and explain something in desperate tones or just flop down himself, mock-relieved. Instead he lies on Deirdre, breathing out each time she breathes in and vice-versa. He smiles as she begins to sing: "Carrot in the wind, carrot in the wind..."

Suddenly the living room opens its mouth and tells of the work of a frail young man of Bangladesh, how he went and went and went until finally he couldn't and simply died, there, in Bangladesh, on the road to riches but no closer to his love, an equally frail young woman named June who lived in Alaska and had seen the young man once on a trip through the East. June died too, the living room says, in a great heap of snow, in winter.

Arch and Czechoslovakia shoot up in surprise and open their mouths simultaneously, then close them, then open them again and scream and scream. Ron comes shooting down the stairs and notices all the guests are gone. Arch and Czechoslovakia notice his nudity and also Deirdre behind him, almost nude. They all stand still and listen. Nothing happens. Someone is going to accuse someone of something. Instead the living room speaks again:

"This is another one, a story about a family's confusion. Why do the family members gawk and not speak? Why do Ron, who was naked with Deirdre, and Arch and Czechoslovakia—why do they not commit themselves to a course of action that will result in something more than the glancing of sport off habit?"

Arch and Ron and Czechoslovakia rebel, declaring their depth and questioning the living room's understanding of their "habit." They walk away through the house, turning off the lights as they go, farther and farther, through more and more rooms, endlessly, turning off lights, farther until they are specks in some very far rooms, still turning off lights, and we see them as just that much more light in the distance—oops! somewhat less—until they vanish utterly, with the very last light, many miles away, at which point they disappear whole into the angry, angry night

"Extra. Connive with the president to extricate his men from junctures. Also, extricate yourself from the big police state. Learn the fashions of diplomacy, learn the suitable face: escape your birth."

Foolish, I had always thought, foolish big-time to poke the laity with a plethora of futures, to rouse their pustulent lives to seepage with these promises and recommendations....

But Mary for the hundredth time thought I was way off base. You never know, she was thinking, who's going to rupture our standards. We list already. The president is losing foot, the garbagemen are screaming in the night, it's all so internal and dense....How else to safeguard the stuff of our poetry and of our souls, our fucking souls, than to learn? Learn learn learn? So we can help the president and through him ourselves?

But learn what? I wondered. Learn about extrication of men? Of oneself from the state? Lacking the state, what have most men got? Minus birth even less. "Escape your birth"—one cringes in embarrassment. There's nothing to learn, it just hurts too much. Give it time.

Mary was getting angry and her thoughts grew jumbled. They can't read our minds, you know. They sit in their chairs and fret because they just don't know what's going on anymore. Could be anything, riflery, non-standard cookery, henchmen, the bizarre....We could be unstable in our traps, we could wreak mongo bad on the funnybone, we could die alone....Don't you feel the winds of anarchy? We have to learn. Imagine if no one at all knows what's going on. Imagine the AIDS. I mean, collectivity isn't working. Collectivity! Maybe in a hundred years, two hundred, we'll be able to sit and spud out, but now it's erudition, honey, it's major lurching for the lobes.

Ach. I was too tired for this work. The individual was all that mattered. Things weren't going to fall apart. The president had his information and the rest was smooth. The tabloids were exploiting us, making us think everything needed us so we'd buy more and more fold-out fret-antifret pills. Maybe in a hundred years, two hundred, the newspapers could be trusted, but for now it had to be all common sense. Sure it was a little dense, a little dark, a little spooky each one sitting alone with his life not knowing much....Men's minds were awry with their openness. It was the gooey dark of it that made the tabloids, which were run by people as fuzzy-minded as the rest of us. People wanted to join up and be concrete.

One couldn't disarm, or detoxify, or burn the books. It was all done. If there were a way to sever one's own head, the cause and center of the new freedom, it would be the most popular thing among the reasonably mature. Mary would be a statistic in a few years. The next generations would consist of those people like me who had once found the act of watching television inexpressibly soothing in its seep of ruthless optimism.

Mary left. I fixed a funny sandwich and laughed as I ate it. The upstairs tenant stomped three times and I laughed some more, then stifled myself in a pillow. Sometime in there I kicked the cat, who bit my leg, which twitched in pain and kicked the cat, who ran. I invented the symphony orchestra, which received a major grant from the president. That humane entity was my friend for sure.

Byway Idylls: Their Possibility and Fun Rather Than Their Frivolity and Ugliness

Mary and Mark descended from the train a ball of fury at the workmen, the stewards, the very conductor in his cell. For hours the train had been lurching and lolling, destroying the calm of babies and breaking up cuddles among the lower-class passengers, and now they were sick. Sick, sick. Sick.

Mary and Mark investigated the station. Cold, and the gravy seemed runny from where they stood across the tray-track. The serving people seemed a little too slick in their stance, too, and that upset our starving heroes in their assumptions. They pranced sultry into the city air and searched the restaurants. Nothing but fastidious gentlemen and grown ladies supping and lunching on special viands, and for what price! So Mary and Mark snaked through the neighborhood; in the wind of the city their stomachs revolted at the scene of trivial splendor and puckered at the call of gilt food, metaphorically.

Soon however they found a butcher's and bought some churning-vittles (pork, yawn, pig-maws) for a gentle stew *a l'ancienne*. They found a disused rattling-can and switched it to their purposes: stew, *a l'ancienne*, gentle. Fervent, too, they set to doing the stew. But the oven was in the gloaming suddenly, it fell on them that nowhere in sight, that awkward, that ugly, and now dusk would fall before they could eat, and they went and bought an oven with a lot of money and then they asked a dozen people, let's say a couple dozen, for an outlet but everyone stood as if naked in the growing gloaming and then finally it happened, they found a special outlet, Mary and Mark, outside a glowing bungalow.

And then, as the men and women passed, and the children too, and also dogs in their many coats, Mary and Mark prepared and settled and all-around busied themselves with the gentle oven as hot, and hotter until soon in the nearly gloaming they'd stewed and eaten and sat and smoked, smoked, smoked. A Mr. Groenbart stopped to chat about the seasoning, which he considered ill-used in this instance, and Mrs. Flee from over the tracks begged for a spoonful for her children—she wanted a taste so she might emulate, in her privacy, for her curious children, the taste of this occasion: the visitors acooking in the bungalow yard.

But then the train tooted and Mary and Mark had to wrench the special spoon from out of the mouth of married Mrs. Flee and charge back, waiting, to the awful, lurching train, which soon was pulling out in its misery on its way to the awful, lurching future of the ride.

RECENT TITLES FROM FICTION COLLECTIVE TWO

Close Your Eyes and Think of Dublin: Portrait of a Girl
A novel by Kathryn Thompson
A brilliant Joycean hallucination of a book in which the richness of
Leopold Bloom's inner life is found in a young American girl experiencing most of the things that vexed James Joyce: sex, church, and
oppression.
197 pages, Cloth: $18.95, Paper: $8.95

Is It Sexual Harassment Yet?
Stories by Cris Mazza
"The stories...continually surprise, delight, disturb, and amuse. Mazza's
'realism' captures the eerie surrealism of violence and repressed
sexuality in her characters' lives."—Larry McCaffery
150 pages, Cloth: $18.95, Paper: $8.95

To Whom It May Concern:
A novel by Raymond Federman
To Whom It May Concern: is not about the Holocaust, it is a book about
the way the Holocaust remains inscribed in the lives of those who
survived. Internationally acclaimed as one of the first postmodernists,
Federman once again has written a captivating novel that raises
questions not only about the Holocaust, but also about the nature and
art of fiction in the post-modernist Holocaust era.
186 pages, Cloth: $18.95, Paper: $8.95

Trigger Dance
Stories by Diane Glancy
"Diane Glancy writes with poetic knowledge of Native Americans...The
characters of *Trigger Dance* do an intricate dance that forms wonderful
new story patterns. With musical language, Diane Glancy teaches us to
hear ancient American refrains amidst familiar American sounds. A
beautiful book."—Maxine Hong Kingston
250 pages, Cloth: $18.95, Paper: $8.95

F/32
A novel by Eurudice Kamvisseli
F/32 is a wild, eccentric, Rabaelaisian romp through most forms of
amorous excess. But, it is also a troubling tale orbiting around a public
sexual assault on the streets of Manhattan. Between the poles of desire
and butchery, the novel and Ela sail, the awed reader going along for
one of the most dazzling rides in recent American fiction.
250 pages, Cloth: $18.95, Paper, $8.95

Between the Flags
Stories by B.H. Friedman
Cool, elegant, and yet surprisingly eccentric, the thirteen stories in
Between the Flags explore contradictions of American experience since
World War II.
189 pages, Cloth: $18.95, Paper: $8.95

In Heaven Everything Is Fine
A novel by Jeffrey DeShell
"As a collage of ill-fated love triangles, this neo-Pop romance may be for
its generation what Barthelme's *Snow White* was for the sixties."—Robert
Steiner
108 pages, Cloth: $18.95, Paper: $8.95

Books may be ordered through the Talman Company, 150 Fifth
Avenue, New York, NY 10011.

FICTION COLLECTIVE TWO
FORTHCOMING TITLES 1991-1992

Double or Nothing, a novel by Raymond Federman

Valentino's Hair, a novel by Yvonne Sapia

Napoleon's Mare, a novella by Lou Robinson

Mermaids for Attila, stories by Jacques Servin

Mabel In Her Twenties, a novel by Rosaire Appel

From the District Files, a novel by Kenneth Bernard